Donut
Shop #9

ILLEGALLY ICED

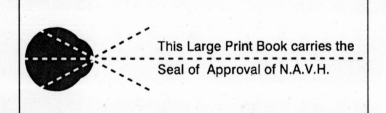

A DONUT SHOP MYSTERY

ILLEGALLY ICED

JESSICA BECK

WHEELER PUBLISHING

A part of Gale, Cengage Learning

GALE
CENGAGE Learning·

Detroit • New York • San Francisco • New Haven, Conn • Waterville, Maine • London

GALE
CENGAGE Learning®

LIBRARY OF CONGRESS CATALOGING-IN-PUBLICATION DATA

Beck, Jessica.
    Illegally Iced : A Donut Shop Mystery / by Jessica Beck. — Large Print edition.
        pages cm. — (Wheeler Publishing Large Print cozy mystery)
        ISBN 978-1-4104-5870-4 (softcover) — ISBN 1-4104-5870-9 (softcover) 1. Coffee shops—Fiction. 2. Private investigators—Fiction. 3. Murder—Investigation—Fiction. 4. North Carolina—Fiction. 5. Large type books. I. Title.
    PS3602.E2693I45 2013
    813'.6—dc23   2013018326

Published in 2013 by arrangement with St. Martin's Press, LLC.

*To everyone who has ever enjoyed
a donut, or one of my mysteries:
Thanks for sharing with me!*

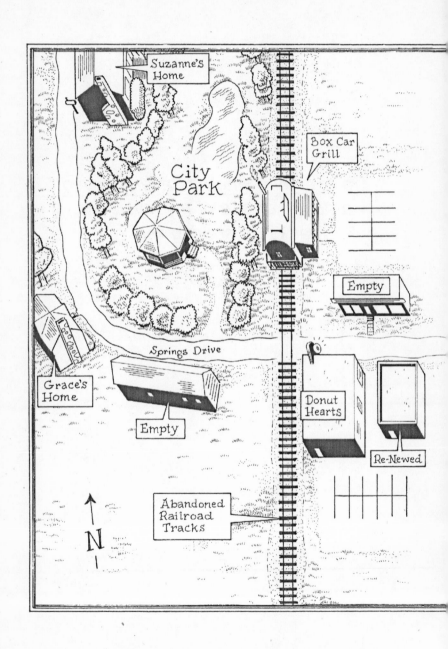

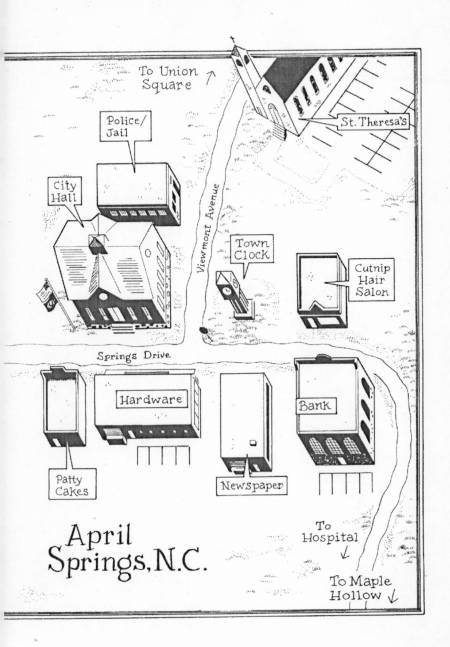

The donut may end, but the hole goes on forever.

— The Author

CHAPTER 1

I heard the woman's scream coming from the park across the street just as I closed the front door of my shop a little after eleven-fifteen on a rare chilly day near the first of May. I was ready for warmer temperatures — along with the rest of April Springs, North Carolina, where I ran Donut Hearts — but the unseasonable cold snap had forced us all into our jackets again. The "Donuts" in the name of my business is pretty self-explanatory, and the "Hearts" part is, too, if you know that my name is Suzanne Hart. I bought the donut place the second my divorce from Max became final, a decision I was normally pretty happy about, but I had to admit that there were a few trying times when I wished I had it all to do over again. That also could be said for moving back in with my mother after my marriage had dissolved, but that's a different thing altogether.

The temperature had been in the low eighties just a few days before, but we'd be lucky to hit the fifties today. The weather hadn't stopped folks from coming out to the park, though. What had that scream been about, anyway? I looked over to see what was going on, but I wasn't too alarmed at first. After all, a great many folks were in the park taking in the sunshine, not seeming to mind the cooler temperatures at all, and I knew there were times when their rambunctiousness got the better of them, kids and adults alike.

After a split second, though, I knew that it hadn't been that kind of scream at all when I heard the next one.

This was a gut-wrenching shriek that shouted, "Something is wrong, something is wrong. Danger. Danger."

I looked up to see two of my favorite customers, Terri Milner and Sandy White, racing toward me with their children in tow. "Suzanne, call 911. Hurry," Sandy said breathlessly as they neared me.

"What happened?" I asked as I reached for my cell phone.

"Somebody just s-t-a-b-b-e-d James Settle." Terri spelled out the crime to soften the blow for her children, but in her shock, she must have forgotten that her twins had learned to spell.

"He was *stabbed*?" one of the little girls asked. "Why would someone do that?"

Terri and Sandy both knelt down and started speaking softly and reassuringly to all three children, trying to calm their obvious distress.

"Is he okay? How bad is it?" I asked them. I couldn't believe it. James Settle and I had gone through a rocky beginning when he'd first come to April Springs, but we'd become good friends since the blacksmith had decided to stay. I couldn't imagine why *anyone* would want to hurt him. I looked wildly around the park and saw a group gathered around something on the ground near the place where he'd been holding his blacksmithing exhibition. Sure enough, it parted for just a moment and I could see our town doctor working on him. I knew at that moment there was nothing I could do to help James.

"I don't know, but it's not good," Terri said sadly, and I felt myself start to react. There were kids there, though, who didn't need to see that, and I had a call to make.

I grabbed my phone from my pocket and dialed a number I knew all too well.

"Grant here," my friend Officer Stephen Grant said as he answered my telephone call; it appeared that he was back on temporary desk duty for another imagined slight on the orders of our chief of police. I was beginning to wonder if Chief Martin was holding his subordinate's friendship with me against him, since he was riding that desk so much lately.

"You need to get over here to the park right away. Someone just stabbed James Settle in front of my shop," I said, trying to shield the phone with my hand so the kids wouldn't have to listen to me repeat what they'd just learned.

"What? Speak up; I can't hear you. Suzanne, is that you?"

I took a few steps away from the group, turned my back to the kids by facing my front store window, and repeated, "Listen, I don't have any more details, but Terri Milner and Sandy White both told me that someone just stabbed James Settle. I don't even know if he's still alive. He was doing a blacksmithing demonstration in the park across from Donut Hearts when I heard the women scream. That's all I know."

"I'll be right there," Officer Grant said.

"Should I call for an ambulance?"

"I'll take care of that myself," he said, and then hung up before I could thank him.

I turned back to the ladies, and saw that

the kids were still really upset by what they'd learned. Who could blame them? It was a pretty horrific thing to learn at such a young age. Maybe there was something that I could do to help, though. "Hey, if you guys are interested, I have some donuts left over from today. Does anybody want a treat, on the house?"

That seemed to get their attention, and I saw the glimmerings of a few smiles.

Just a few seconds earlier, Emma had walked outside to see what the commotion was all about, and she looked at me oddly as I made the offer, not knowing what had just happened.

"Something just happened to James Settle, and everyone's really upset. Do you mind helping out and waiting on them? Give them whatever they want. I'll fill you in with all of the details later."

"I'm glad to do it," she answered. Ever since she'd come back to town and was working for me again, Emma had become the model employee. College life away from home hadn't agreed with her, and she was truly excited to get her old life back.

As Emma unlocked the door and led them all inside, Terri turned to me and mouthed the word, "Thanks."

I nodded and said softly, "You're welcome," as she and Sandy — along with their children — walked into Donut Hearts. I noticed a few other kids who were hiding between their parents' legs in the general vicinity, and I walked around and repeated the offer to all of them I could find. We had about three dozen donuts left from the day's sales, and I was glad we had them. These kids needed a good memory to help blunt the bad one they were all sharing now. By the time I'd escorted the last of them discreetly into the shop, Officer Grant drove up. I saw that Chief Martin was sitting beside him, so evidently the banishment had been lifted, at least for the moment.

As they approached me, I couldn't help noticing how the chief's former bulk had diminished even more than the last time I'd seen him. Since the man had been dating my mother, he'd constantly been on a killer diet and exercise plan, and it showed. I wasn't sure how far he was going to take it. I liked carrying a few extra pounds around on my frame — or so I lied to myself whenever I passed by a mirror — unlike my best friend, Grace Gauge. She could still fit into her prom dress, while I probably wouldn't even be able to belt my oversized robe from high school around my waist these days.

"What exactly happened here?" the police chief asked me.

"I have no idea," I said, happy for once that I wasn't involved in any way, shape, or form.

"But you called the stabbing in," he said, clearly a little confused by my denial.

"I didn't see a thing. Terri Milner and Sandy White asked me to call you for them," I admitted.

"Then where are they?"

I pointed behind me into the donut shop. "They're having donuts with their kids. They were all pretty traumatized by what happened. If you're looking for James, he's over there. Doc's trying to do what he can for him." Just then I heard a siren's wail in the background, and I knew that the paramedics were on their way.

Chief Martin stared at me a second, shook his head, and then turned to his subordinate. "Grant, take Lincoln and secure the perimeter."

"Yes, sir," Grant said as he happily hurried into action, joining up with another officer who was doing his best to keep the growing crowd away from the blacksmith so that the doctor could work on him.

The police chief was about to join him when he turned back to me and said, "Suzanne, I'd appreciate it if you wouldn't go anywhere."

"I'm not sure what else I can tell you, but I'll be in the shop until you need me," I said, and then I started back into Donut Hearts.

"Hey, are the free donuts I've been hearing about available to everyone?" a big, husky man asked me before I could get back inside the donut shop. He must have heard someone say that I was giving them away.

"That depends," I asked. "Are you so scared right now that you need your mommy to comfort you?"

He shook his head. "No, I can't say that I am."

"Then come back tomorrow," I said as I patted his arm. "You can have one then."

He smiled. "Hey, there's no harm in asking, right?"

I liked the way he took the rejection, so I added, "If you do decide to come in tomorrow and ask for me, you can have one donut on the house."

"That sounds good." He smiled a bit too strongly at me as he added, "Maybe I can take you out for lunch tomorrow after you finish working."

"That would be great," I said with a false smile. "My boyfriend's a state police inspector, and I expect him back in town tonight. We can both be ready about noon."

"Did I say tomorrow?" he quickly back-pedaled. "What was I thinking? I just remembered that I'm going to be out of town all day tomorrow."

"How about a rain check, then?" I asked innocently.

"I'll let you know," he said, and then took off quickly down the street.

I looked over and saw the chief trying to stop folks from leaving the crime scene, but he wasn't having much luck. Finally, he pulled a whistle out of his front shirt pocket and blew it shrilly.

Everyone stopped dead in their tracks.

"Stay right where you are," he said with all of the authority he possessed. As he said it, I noticed that three other officers were just arriving on the scene. That left just one cop to cover the rest of April Springs, but it was understandable. Murder didn't visit our sleepy little town every day, and whenever it did, it always threw everything off kilter until the killer was finally caught. "I've got an officer coming around to take your names and contact information. Be prepared to show your ID as well. Anyone without an ID will be asked to stay behind until we can determine if you're really who

19

you say you are."

An older woman near him said quite clearly, "Phillip Martin, my driver's license is at home, along with my car keys. I'm eighty-seven years old, and I knew your father and his father before him. Are you telling me that I can't leave this chilly park and find some comfort by my fireplace at home?"

"No, that's fine, Mrs. Jenkins. You can go."

Before the rest of them could come up with excuses of their own, the chief added, "Okay, if you're over eighty-five, you can take off. Everyone else needs to stick around, though."

Mrs. Jenkins paused as she walked past me and offered me a quick wink. I smiled slightly as I returned it, and then watched her walk away without the slightest catch in her step.

As the chief and his men started taking names, a voice behind me asked sweetly, "Suzanne Hart, what kind of trouble have you gotten yourself into this time?"

Though he'd tried to disguise it, there was no way that I wouldn't know Jake's voice. I turned to my boyfriend and hugged him with a great deal more force than I'd intended. I'd been holding it together for the sake of everyone else around me, but having Jake there to lean on allowed me to let some of it go. "It's just awful," I said as the words poured out of me. "Someone just stabbed James Settle."

"I heard about it on the radio on my way over here," he answered. "How bad is it?"

"They're still working on him," I said as I glanced over in that direction.

"My timing's pretty lousy, isn't it?"

I hugged him tighter. "Never, ever apologize for coming to see me," I said. "How long can you stay this time?" His job investigating significant crime took him all over the state of North Carolina, and I was lucky to see him once a month, not that I was complaining. I didn't need to be courted and pampered seven days a week, but when Jake *could* make it to April Springs I had to fight from declaring a donut holiday so I could spend more time with him.

"I don't have much time at all," he admitted sadly. "Are you free for dinner?"

"Why wait that long? We can start with lunch and work our way up to dinner," I said. "I'm really glad that you're here. Give me a second and then we can go." I suddenly remembered Chief Martin's instructions to me before he'd left. "Shoot. The chief asked me to hang around until after he was finished."

"Do you know anything about what happened?" Jake asked, his gaze lingering over the crime scene.

"I heard two screams, and then a pair of my customers ran over here with their kids and asked me to call 911. That's the sum total of everything I know."

He nodded gravely. "Then you should be in the clear."

"Maybe," I said a little reluctantly.

"What does that mean?"

"James and I had a disagreement about the smoke from his portable fire pit coming into my shop this morning, but it was really nothing."

"Is that what he was using for a forge?"

"Of course not," I said. James had given me a crash course in blacksmithing several months before, and I'd remembered quite a few things about it. "That fire would never get hot enough for forging, but he told me that he wanted the folks who lingered to watch to stay warm, so he brought the pit along as well. That's where all the smoke was coming from."

"Okay. Let me talk to the chief and see if I can get you excused."

I glanced back inside and said, "If you'd like, I can go with you. Give me a second to talk to Emma, and then we can both tell the chief I'm leaving." I glanced over at Jake and saw that his attention was still focused on the crime scene. I doubted that he'd heard a word I'd said. "Would you rather postpone lunch and go talk to Chief Martin yourself first? I don't mind if that's what you want to do; really I don't."

He kissed me quickly, and then said, "Thanks. I won't be long," as he hurried toward the action while everyone else with the slightest bit of sense was doing their best to get away from it.

I walked into my donut shop and saw that nearly all of our leftover donuts had been consumed by our makeshift crowd. A great deal of the tension I'd seen earlier had begun to ease. I knew that my meager offerings wouldn't erase what they'd seen, but at least it might help them forget, at least for a moment or two.

"Is everyone feeling better?" I asked.

As though they were all in school, the kids turned to me en masse and said in a semblance of unison, "Thank you, Mrs. Hart."

"Actually, you can all call me Suzanne," I said. A few of the mothers noticed the familiarity, but I didn't care. I wanted these kids to feel safe and welcome in my shop, and if I stepped on a few adult toes doing it, so be it.

"What do we owe you?" Sandy asked as she approached me, digging into her huge purse.

"Don't worry about it. It's on the house," I said, making it loud enough for everyone to hear.

"But we had chocolate milk, too," she protested. "The donuts may have been extras, but the milks weren't."

"Leave something in the tip jar if you feel like you have to and we'll be square," I said. I'd originally put it there to help Emma with her college expenses, but now that she was living at home again I'd have to find another way to put it to good use. I just knew that I wouldn't feel right keeping it for myself, or even splitting it with my assistant. There were no worries, though. I was certain that I'd find a good cause for it if I just put my mind to it.

I saw that Jake was back, but he didn't come inside. I stepped out, and the second I saw his face, I knew that it was bad news.

"He's dead, isn't he?" I asked.

"I'm sorry, Suzanne."

I felt something inside die a little. "Do they have any idea who might have done it?"

He shook his head, and I felt a rage begin to boil for whoever had taken my friend away from all of us.

"The chief needs me over there, but I thought you should know," he said as he gave me a tender hug before he left.

When I walked back inside, I did my best to smile, even though I was shattered by the unbelievable news. "If we're all finished eating, I'd appreciate it if you all would do something for me," I asked loudly.

"Anything," Terri said. "Just name it. Would you like Sandy and me to stay behind and help clean up?"

"That won't be necessary, but thanks for the offer."

"Then what can we do?" Sandy asked.

"I want you all to go out and try to have a lovely afternoon," I said with my brightest smile. It was tough to do, but the kids deserved it.

It was a relief to see so many smiles coming back at me. I was in shock about James's murder, and I knew that the truth of the matter was that it hadn't even hit me yet, but I had made up my mind to be brave for these kids, and I was going to do exactly that, even if it crushed me. A few mothers visited the tip jar, though I couldn't see what they were contributing, nor did I care.

After they were all gone, Emma said, "I'll get started on these dishes."

I shook my head as I said, "Don't worry about it. I'll be happy to do them myself. Emma, thanks for sticking around to help out. I appreciate it."

"Is it really true? How is James doing?" she asked earnestly.

"I'm afraid that he's dead," I answered. I looked around the dining area, and realized that the mess might be exactly what I needed to take my mind off what had just happened. "Now take off before I change my mind."

She was gone in an instant, and I locked the door behind her.

In fifteen minutes I had the dishes done, the floor swept, *and* the counter and table-tops wiped down, but there was still no sign of Jake. I decided not to wait for him in the shop, since a few folks had already come by and knocked to get in while I'd been cleaning up. There were two donuts left, both in the heart shape of a cutter I'd gotten from my temporary employee, Nan Winters, and I'd saved them just for him. He hadn't had one of the new shapes of donut yet, and I wanted him to get at least one while he was in town.

I took a seat at the table out in front of the shop and watched the police move with amazing efficiency as they examined the crime scene. James's body was gone, but his portable blacksmithing equipment was still there — and his fire pit as well, still sending up wisps of smoke every now and then. Why would someone want to kill him? It had to have been a heated argument, no pun intended. After all, it wasn't likely that someone had planned to stab him in broad daylight in the park with dozens of eyewitnesses around. That meant that it was either done in a burst of passion, or because the opportunity presented itself. Whoever had killed him had the guts of a cat burglar, and I didn't envy the police chief as he tried to catch the culprit.

I was still waiting for Jake when I noticed someone walking toward me from the storefront closest to mine.

What did Gabby Williams want with me, and why did she look so upset?

I had a feeling that I was about to find out, and what was more, I was pretty sure that I wasn't going to like it. I had to fight the impulse to run away in the opposite direction the second I saw her bearing down on me, but I held my ground as she neared me.

"I just don't understand it. Why did you have to kill him, Suzanne?" Gabby shouted as she got closer, and I knew that my initial instincts to escape had been right on the money.

I wasn't sure why Gabby was accusing me of murder, but I knew that I had to nip it in the bud before the story spread all over April Springs. I'd been convicted in the court of public opinion before, and I had no desire to ever revisit the experience again.

FRIED CINNAMON TOAST

This is a variation on one of our old camping favorites. Instead of cooking the dough on a stick over a campfire, though, we load it down with our delicious extras and deep-fry it. One of my best, and easiest, donut recipes! This one is well worth a try!

Ingredients
- 1 canister refrigerated biscuits (we use Pillsbury Grands! Homestyle Buttermilk in the 10.2 oz. size with 5 biscuits)

Mixed
- 3/4 cup sugar, white granulated
- 1/2 stick butter, softened (4 tablespoons)
- 1 1/2 tablespoons cinnamon

- Canola oil for frying (the amount depends on your pot or fryer)

Instructions
Open the canister of biscuits and pat in your hands until they are in oval shapes. Mix the softened butter, sugar, and cinnamon, and then put 1 to 2 tablespoons in the center of the oval. Bring the dough up around the sides and pinch the edges tightly.

Drop the logs of dough into the oil, being

careful not to splash hot oil. Fry in the hot canola oil (360 to 370 degrees F) 3 to 5 minutes, turning halfway through. Remove when they're golden brown, and you'll be greeted with five cinnamon smiles!

Yield: 5 cinnamon toast sticks

CHAPTER 2

"What are you talking about? Have you lost your mind? *I* didn't kill him," I said angrily, my temper flaring despite my best effort to keep it in check.

"I heard you two fighting not two hours ago," Gabby said, "so don't try to deny it. Suzanne, I'm not saying that you didn't have a right to be angry with the man, but you shouldn't have killed him."

We were starting to gather a bit of crowd now ourselves. I had to find a way to shut Gabby up, and quick. "I didn't touch him," I said, this time letting my voice grow louder by the second. The sooner I could dispel Gabby's theory in everyone's minds, the better off I'd be.

"I know what I saw, so don't bother trying to deny that you were arguing with him this morning, Suzanne."

I was about to answer when I saw Chief Martin approach us with Jake on his heels.

Oh, boy.

Now I was in the thick of it whether I wanted to be or not.

"Tell me exactly what happened this morning, Suzanne," Chief Martin said. "I thought you said earlier that you didn't know anything about the murder."

"I didn't do it!" I repeated loudly for everyone's benefit. I was about to add something else when I saw Jake shake his head slightly. It was clear that he didn't want me explaining myself too much when I was angry, and most likely with good reason. I had a tendency to share too much when I was in trouble, and I wouldn't be doing myself any favors at the moment if I kept talking.

"I never said that you did," the chief said patiently, and I was happy that I'd heeded Jake's advice. "But," Chief Martin added, "if what Gabby Williams just said is true, you had a confrontation with the man this morning, and now he's dead. You have to admit that it doesn't look good for you, Suzanne."

"It wasn't anything like a *confrontation*," I said, stressing the last word as I stared hard at Gabby. To her credit, she didn't even flinch. I thought we'd worked out our tenuous friendship over the past few years, but evidently that extended only so far with Gabby.

"Then what was it?" the chief asked. I looked at Jake, who encouraged me with a subtle nod to explain it to the chief of police.

"It was more like a conversation," I amended.

"About what, exactly?" he asked.

Jake made a rolling motion with his fingers, telling me that it was okay to elaborate.

I knew that it wasn't going to sound too good for me, but it was the truth, and I had to tell it. "The smoke from his fire pit was coming into the donut shop, and I asked him as nicely as I could to move it somewhere else."

"And what did he say?" the chief asked.

"He told me that he was sorry, but he couldn't do anything about it since there was already a fire going in it, and then he went back to work," I admitted.

"I bet that steamed you pretty good," the chief said.

"Hey, that's enough of that," Jake said, finally speaking up.

The chief didn't apologize, though. He simply shrugged at Jake, looked back at me, and then said, "You know that we'll talk more about this later, right?"

I just nodded, not trusting myself to speak. I knew that tone of voice too well, since I'd heard it often enough in the past from him. I was becoming a person of interest in his mind, no matter what his relationship might be with my mother, and I didn't care for it, not one single bit. It appeared that no matter how unwilling I was to investigate another murder, if the chief's attitude was any indication of what the entire town might be thinking at the moment, I really wasn't going to have much choice.

I was going to have to figure out who killed James Settle myself.

"We might as well get it over with now," I told the chief. "Do we have to go downtown, or will a table at the donut shop do?"

"Your shop is fine," he said.

Jake started to follow us, but Chief Martin shook his head. "I'm sorry, but this is a private conversation."

"Either I go with her or she gets a lawyer," Jake said in his best authoritative voice.

The police chief shook his head and tried his best to calm my boyfriend down. "That just makes her look guilty, and we both know it. I shouldn't have to explain that to you."

Jake wasn't about to take that, not even from his friend. "Chief," he said, stressing the man's title, "Suzanne has every right to be represented. If that makes her seem guilty in your mind, then that says more about you than it does about her."

I had to stop this before it went any further. I knew how it could be when two people with stubborn streaks started butting heads. After all, Momma and I had played out that kind of scene ourselves too many times to count.

I turned to Jake and patted his shoulder. "It won't take long. I'll be fine."

"I still don't like it," Jake said, continuing to stare at the chief.

I was about to say something when Chief Martin surprised us all by saying in a soft voice, "Jake, I respect the fact that you're looking out for Suzanne's best interests, but how is it going to look if I don't talk to her right away? Everyone in town knows that I'm dating her mother. If I give her a free pass on this, it's going to look bad for all three of us. You can see that, can't you?"

"Does that mean that you don't think I killed James?" I asked.

"I'm sorry, but I'm not willing to say that just yet." He then contradicted himself by adding softly so that no one around us could hear, "Of course I don't believe it for one second, but I have to gather evidence as though I didn't know you."

I knew it couldn't have been easy for the chief to say that, and I had to admit that it made me feel quite a bit better. "Jake, I'm going to talk to him alone."

My boyfriend thought about it, and then nodded. "Okay, but try to curb that habit you have of overexplaining everything," he added with a grin.

"I'll do what I can, but I'm not making any promises."

The chief and I walked into the shop, and I said, "I'd offer you coffee, but I just dumped the last of it down the sink. Should I put another pot on for you and your men?"

"Thanks, but we'll be fine. Now," he said as he took out his notebook, "tell me everything."

"I just did," I said.

"Indulge me, Suzanne."

His pen didn't move until I was willing to start talking, so I told him everything about my interaction with James again, and then once more.

"That's all well and good," he said after finishing the last note. "And after your conversation, did you speak with him again?"

"No. I couldn't. I was working the front of the shop by myself, and I never heard a thing about what happened until I was locking up for the day."

"Can Emma verify that?" he asked.

"No, she was in back."

"Can anyone, then? Think hard. It could be important."

"I'm trying, but there's no one that I can think of." And then I remembered Harry Dale. The man had come in with me after I'd spoken to James about his fire, and then he'd proceeded to nurse his coffee until I had to throw him out just before the mothers asked me to call the police. I'd resented him taking up my best couch for so long, but I was so happy that I could kiss the man right now. "Talk to Harry Dale. He sat right over there the entire time, from my conversation with James to the time just before Sandy and Terri showed up."

Chief Martin chuckled a little, clearly relieved by the news. "Harry does tend to nest, doesn't he? I'll give him a call, and then you should be in the clear."

"Maybe with you, but I've got a feeling that the rest of April Springs is going to be harder to convince."

The police chief nodded in instant sympathy and understanding. "Folks do tend to believe the worst about people sometimes, don't they?"

"When murder's involved? You can count on it every time," I said.

"Let me call Harry, and then we'll see what we can do."

He stepped away and grabbed his radio — no doubt to get Harry's telephone number — while I swept the same part of our floor over and over again. Surely my customer would back up my story. But what if he didn't? No, I couldn't think like that. I wasn't going to even entertain the possibility that he wouldn't verify what I'd just told the chief. I glanced outside a full minute later and saw Jake staring inside the donut shop impatiently.

I held my hands up, trying to signify that he should be patient, but there was nothing else I could do to ease his concern.

I heard the police chief talking on his phone in the corner, and after a full minute, he smiled as he hung up. "You're in the clear, Suzanne. You'll be happy to know that Harry backs up your story one hundred percent."

"Good for him," I said with a grin of my own. "Does that mean that I can go back outside now?"

"Lead the way," he said.

Once we were on the sidewalk in front of the donut shop again, he turned to me and said loudly, "Your alibi holds up, Suzanne. You're in the clear. There's no way you could have stabbed James Settle."

"Thank you," I said, and then winked at him when I was sure that no one could see me.

After Chief Martin crossed the street and returned to the crime scene, Jake rejoined me. "How did you manage to do that?"

"What are you talking about?" I asked with a grin.

"He was really looking out for you just then, wasn't he? I owe the man an apology. I probably shouldn't have butted in like that."

"Jake, I appreciate you standing up for me, but you know that I can handle things by myself."

He wrapped his arms around me. "Suzanne, there are times when it makes perfectly good sense to be independent, but you don't *always* have to do everything on your own."

"I don't," I said as I squeezed him a little hard before I let him go. "After all, I've got Grace, don't I?"

"Among others," he said with a twinkle strong in his eyes.

"Do you mean like Momma and George?" I asked, barely able to suppress my smile.

He kissed me, and then said, "Don't push your luck. You know I'll do whatever I can to help you. Do you want me to try to get out of this assignment? If you need my help investigating James's murder, I'll find a way to make it happen."

I loved the fact that Jake knew me so well. There was no way I was going to walk away without trying to figure out who had killed James. "No. As much as I appreciate the offer, I'll be fine with the reserves that I have in my corner now." Almost as an afterthought, I added, "If I get in too deep, though, I may have to take you up on your offer."

"That's my girl."

I was far from being a "girl" by just about anyone's definition, but I liked the way it sounded when Jake said it.

"Now, I distinctly remember something about you promising me lunch, right?"

He laughed at the reminder, a sound that I dearly loved. "Name the place, and if I can afford it, you can order whatever you want on the menu."

"Oh, this is going to cost you."

"Where should we go?" he asked.

"I was thinking we could walk over to the Boxcar," I said, pointing to the restaurant just across the road.

"Are you sure that's not too close to the park?" Jake asked.

"You mean the spot where James was murdered?"

"I do," he admitted.

"Thanks for thinking of me, but I can't let that dictate what I do. If I let it stop me now, when will I ever be able to go to Trish's again? It might not be easy, but I'd rather face it right now."

"At least let me hold your hand as we walk," he said. It was one of Jake's increasing public shows of affection, and at the moment, I was doubly glad for it.

"It's a deal," I said as I slipped my hand in his. I tried to avoid staring at the tape cordoning off the crime scene as we neared it, but it was impossible. James's fire had finally gone out, but his tools were still arrayed in front of his anvil. It looked as though he'd stepped away for a second and would be right back, but I knew that wasn't ever going to happen. He'd become a presence in April Springs since he'd first come to town coveting our abandoned railroad tracks, but we'd worked that out long ago. I had a set of iron railroad track bookends he'd made for me from a different supply of rails, and they sat proudly on my desk. James and I had become friends since then, sharing time and enjoying the odd mix of characters that made up our little town together. I would miss him. In most folks' minds, it might not have been much of a reason to throw myself into a murder investigation, but it was enough for me.

I was going to do my best to find the killer and avenge my friend's death.

"Hi, Suzanne," Trish said sadly as Jake and I walked into the diner. Her eyes were bloodshot, and it was clear that she'd been crying. "I'm so glad to see you." As she hugged me, I saw her ponytail bob slightly, a trademark of hers since high school. She and Grace were two of my best friends in the world, and I loved them both dearly. I hated to see her so upset. As she pulled away, she dabbed at her eyes as she said, "Poor James. Who could have done such a terrible thing to him?"

"I have no idea," I answered. It had hit her harder than I would have expected. Had she been that close to James, or was it the proximity of the murder that had shaken her so much?

"I hate to interrupt," Jake said with a smile, "but I want every second I can get with you, Suzanne."

"I understand completely," Trish said as

she seated Jake and me at a table near the register. She wiped at her eyes and, pointing to the menus, asked, "Do you even need those?"

"No, we're good," I said, and then glanced at Jake. "You know what you're having for lunch, right?"

Jake pushed the menu away. "I trust your judgment, so I'll just have whatever you're having."

Trish's eyebrows shot up. "What?" Jake asked. "Did I say something stupid?"

"It's just a dangerous thing to offer," Trish said, trying her best to cheer herself up. "You'd better hope that Suzanne takes it easy on you."

I considered it for a second as I pondered my choices, and then finally told Trish, "We'll have two cheeseburgers all the way, a big basket of onion rings, and a pair of Cokes." After I'd ordered, I turned to Jake and asked, "How does that sound to you?"

"Like I just got off too easy," he admitted.

"I can be quite a bit more daring if you're really game," I said.

"No, I wasn't complaining. Cheeseburgers sound great to me."

Trish shook her head as she jotted down the order. "You're getting soft, Suzanne."

"I know," I acknowledged. "What can I say?"

"You don't need to say a thing. It's written all over your face," Trish replied.

I looked back at Jake to find him studying me intently.

"What are you looking at?"

"I don't see it," he said gravely.

"What?"

"What's written on your face."

I smiled at him. "It's love, you big goof."

"Oh, so *that*'s what that is," he replied, grinning broadly at me. "I suppose I have some of that on my face as well."

Our sodas arrived, and then in short order, our food. Jake and I tried not to talk too much about business — especially if it involved crime — while we were eating, but it wasn't always easy to do.

We were just finishing up when his cell phone rang. He glanced at the number, clearly ready to dismiss it, and then he saw who it was. "I have to take this. It's my boss," he said. "I'm sorry."

As Jake held a muted conversation, I looked around the Boxcar and saw that several people were studying me covertly. The moment our gazes met, each one looked quickly away. That wasn't the way most folks treated someone they thought of as innocent. If there had been any doubt in my mind before about investigating James's murder, it was all gone now. Whether I liked it or not, I was clearly guilty until proven innocent.

Jake was not happy when he ended his call and put his phone away.

"Was it bad news?" I asked.

"I can't believe that I'm doing this, but I have to leave right now. I was hoping to wait until tomorrow, but evidently it's more urgent than I was led to believe at first. Do you mind?"

"It's your job. Go on," I said. "I'll take care of the check."

"You got it the last time, and besides, I'm not in *that* big of a hurry." Jake took a twenty out of his wallet and threw it down on the table before kissing me briefly. "I'll call you tonight," he said, and then he was gone.

Trish came out of the kitchen just in time to see him leave. "Is he coming back?" she asked.

"His boss just called," I said. "He had to go."

I handed Trish the money. "Keep the change," I said.

She whistled softly. "That's a nice tip."

"If it's too much, you can always bring

the two of us some pie to make up the difference," I replied straight-faced.

"Do you know what? That sounds like a
great idea," Trish said. "I need to talk to
you." Thirty seconds later she was back with
two slices of apple pie, each topped with
vanilla ice cream.

"Will the extra tip really cover all of that?"
I asked as she slid one piece in front of me
and kept the other piece for herself.

"Don't ask questions and just dig in."

"Those are orders I'm happy to follow
anytime," I admitted as I took my first bite.
I would never tell Momma, but Trish's pies
easily rivaled her own.

As we ate, I asked Trish, "What did you
want to talk about?"

She started to tell me, and then the tears
began again.

I reached out and touched her hand.
"Trish, are you okay?"

"Not so much," and before I could ask
her anything else, she stood up abruptly and
ducked back into the kitchen. This was
forbidden territory for anyone but her staff,
but I knew that I couldn't just let her walk
away from me. Something was troubling
her, and I needed to know if I could help.

I waited nearly a full minute, and then she
came out again. "Sorry about that," she said.

"Trish, what's going on?"

"I was wrong before. I can't talk about it, Suzanne, at least not right now, so please don't ask me."

"Are you sure?"

"Absolutely, but thanks for caring."

I knew when it was time to drop it. If and when Trish was ready to talk to me, I'd be there for her, but in the meantime, the worst thing I could do was push her if she wasn't ready to talk yet. I tried to leave another tip to cover my portion of pie, but Trish wouldn't let me get away with it. "Are you *trying* to hurt my feelings?" she asked the second she spotted the money.

"We both know that I would never knowingly do that," I said as I took it back.

A teenager came to the register with his bill and said, "I don't want to hurt your feelings, either. Should I just keep this, too?"

Trish snatched the cash out of his hand and rang up the sale. "You'd be amazed at how thick a skin I have sometimes, Tommy Jenkins."

As I left the diner, I was still worried about my friend, but what made it even worse was when I spotted the crime scene tape again.

I knew that I had to deal with the blacksmith's murder, but there was something even more urgent that I needed to do at that moment.

I had to confront Gabby Williams about what she thought she'd seen before the entire town heard her rendition of what had happened earlier with James Settle. I wasn't at all certain that I could get her to see the truth about what she'd witnessed, but I owed it to myself to at least try.

KOOL-AID CAKE BITES

When I heard about these donuts being served at our county fair, I had to try my own recipe. The taste, as well as the color, is BOLD! We love these, so if you're feeling adventurous one day, try them!

Ingredients

Mixed
- 1 egg, lightly beaten
- 3/4 cup sugar, white granulated
- 2 tablespoons butter, melted
- 1 teaspoon vanilla extract

Sifted
- 2 cups flour, unbleached all-purpose
- 1 full packet of powdered unsweetened Kool-Aid mix, .13 oz. (we like Tropical Punch!)
- 1 tablespoon baking powder
- Dash of salt

- Canola oil for frying (the amount depends on your pot or fryer)

Instructions

In one bowl, beat the egg lightly, and then add the sugar, butter, and vanilla. In a separate bowl, sift together the flour, Kool-

Aid packet, baking powder, and salt.

Add the dry ingredients to the wet, mixing well until you have a smooth consistency. It's fun to do this one with your kids, because when you mix the dry and wet together, the colors go from bland to BRIGHT!

Drop bits of dough using a small-sized cookie scoop (the size of your thumb, approximately). Fry in hot canola oil (360 to 370 degrees F) 1 1/2 to 2 minutes, turning halfway through.

Yield: 10–12 donut holes

CHAPTER 3

"Gabby, we need to talk," I called out as I saw her duck back into her secondhand clothing shop, ReNEWed.

"Suzanne, I don't have anything to say to you," she answered as she slammed the door to her shop in my face.

This woman had clearly lost her mind. "Gabby, you know me," I said through the door, hoping that she was still just on the other side of it. "Think about it. If the police believe me when I say that I'm innocent, how can you possibly think that I could have done it?"

There was no response, and though I hated to play the next card, I really had no choice. Gabby was influential in our town, and I couldn't afford to be on her bad side. "Let me ask you something. Who stood by you the last time you were accused of murder, when most of the other folks in April Springs turned their backs on you?"

There was a pause, and then I heard the dead bolt unlock. Gabby opened the door and then stepped to one side so I could come in. I felt a little better being inside her shop, but I noticed that she still had her cell phone in one hand. Was she preparing to call the police at a moment's notice? All around us, Gabby had the usual array of beautiful clothing for sale, but I wasn't there to browse.

"You were always on my side," she reluctantly admitted. "But that doesn't change what happened this morning, Suzanne. I saw what I saw."

"But did you really? Sure, James and I were talking about the smoke from his fire coming into my shop, but we weren't yelling at each other, were we?"

She considered it, and then shook her head. "Maybe not, but you can't deny that you weren't very happy with him."

"Of course I can't," I said. "But we were friends. He explained to me that he couldn't move his fire pit without risking burning the park down, and I went back into my shop when I understood that he couldn't make my problem go away. At no time after that did I ever approach him or even say another word to him, let alone stab him." I knew that Gabby had her finger on the pulse of the town, and if I asked her the next question on my mind, it was more than likely that she'd be able to answer it, and it might even distract her for a second. "Have you heard yet exactly *what* James was stabbed with?"

"One of his wrought-iron skewers," Gabby said, clearly pleased to have the information before I did. "Evidently he'd just made it this morning."

"How can they be sure of that? I have a couple of his skewers in the donut shop myself." I'd experimented with using them to flip the donuts in the fryer halfway through their cooking cycles, but I'd quickly gone back to my old reliable method of using thick wooden chopsticks instead. As a matter of fact, the skewers were both still in one of my kitchen drawers. Would that help my cause, or put me into deeper trouble?

"What do the ends of them look like?" she asked.

I thought about the long and thin black iron tapers and the boxed ends that made them easier to hold. "They are both diamond-shaped," I admitted. "Why do you ask?"

"Then you really should be in the clear. These had curlicue circles at the top, and he told me that he'd just started using the new pattern today and was still experimenting with the design."

That was an interesting fact. "When did he tell you that?"

"I walked over to his demonstration when he first got started this morning," Gabby admitted. "I've always liked James, and I wanted to say good morning to him."

That particular friendship was news to me. "Really?"

She must have sensed something in my voice. "Yes, really. Is it that hard to believe that a handsome young man would find pleasure in my company?"

I couldn't stop myself from blurting out, "Are you telling me that the two of you were *dating*?"

"Of course not." She looked flustered by the question. "I commissioned him to make me a set of those handsome bookends out of railroad tracks like he made you. I've admired them since you got a set yourself. Unfortunately, he never got around to making a pair for me."

"Gabby, I'm so sorry. I didn't mean to imply . . ."

She stepped in when I failed to come up with the words to explain just what I had been trying to say. "It's all right, Suzanne. I don't have that many friends left these days, and I just lost one of them. Now that I think about it, I believe you when you say that you didn't do anything to James. I know that you two were friends as well, even if you were having a rocky time of it today." She paused, and then looked sad. "What were your last words to him, do you remember?"

I wasn't ever going to forget them. "I told him that if it ever happened again, he'd have to go to Hickory for his donuts for the rest of his life."

"How dreadful."

"Honestly, it could have been a great deal worse," I said. "At least I smiled when I said it."

"I myself told him how lucky we all were to have him living in April Springs. He seemed pleased by the compliment."

"I'm sure that he was," I answered, though I wondered if that was really what Gabby had told him. "So, we're good, right?"

"Right as rain," she said.

"Excellent," I said. "I can't tell you what a relief that is. Gabby, you must know that your opinion is very important to me."

The woman actually looked pleased by my confession. "I feel the same way about you. Let's forget this ever happened. Agreed?"

"Agreed," I said, and on an impulse that I couldn't name, I stepped forward and hugged her. It was clear by her stiffness that she wasn't all that used to being embraced, so I released her almost immediately.

Things were awkward as our gazes met again, and Gabby said, "Suzanne, I can't just stand around and chat with you all day. I've got work to do. Not all of us have such flexible hours that we're off every day before the crack of noon."

My first impulse was to argue with her about her blanket — and completely wrong — statement, but I bit back the impulse with all my might. I came into my shop at three a.m. every day, seven days a week. I was many things in this world, but lazy wasn't one of them.

When Gabby saw that she wasn't going to get a rise out of me, she smiled for a split second and then watched me walk out of her shop.

At least I'd been able to persuade her that I was innocent. I hoped so, at any rate. For now, though, I could put her out of my mind with a big check mark beside her name. It was just one of many things that I hoped to accomplish today, but it was an important one, and I was glad that I'd been able to talk to her before the wrong ideas were so ingrained in her mind that she'd never be able to change her opinion about my innocence.

As I started back toward Donut Hearts, I noticed that someone was leaving a note on the windshield of my Jeep. That could have meant that I'd been dinged during a misguided parking attempt, or perhaps they were leaving a pamphlet or an announcement that I wouldn't be interested in.

It was neither of those things, though, and I was happy when I saw who it was.

I hurried toward Grace and said loudly, "Grace, over here."

She turned toward the direction of my voice, and I saw my best friend — pretty and blond and slim — smile at me. "There you are. I've been looking all over town for you. Where have you been hiding?"

"I was talking to Gabby at ReNEWed," I said.

Grace laughed a little. "Okay, I admit that I wasn't desperate enough to look for you in there. How *is* Gabby, anyway?"

"Earlier this morning she was accusing me of murder, but I managed to talk my way out of it."

Grace studied me for a moment, perhaps waiting for my smile to acknowledge that I was just kidding, but when it wasn't forthcoming, she asked haltingly, "Murder? Who was killed?"

"You haven't heard? Someone stabbed James Settle in the park a little while ago."

"That's terrible," Grace said, the life going out of her for a moment. "What a waste." She paused, and then asked, "Why did Gabby think you might have done it?"

"James and I were arguing about smoke coming into my shop this morning, and we had a few words, all friendly enough, but Gabby misunderstood. The second she heard what happened, she started singing her head off."

"Suzanne, are you in trouble?"

"Not with the police. I have a pretty solid alibi, and Chief Martin has already confirmed it. Harry Dale was in the donut shop drinking free coffee all morning."

Grace nodded slightly. "You were lucky he was there. Does that mean that we aren't going to investigate his murder?" My best friend and I had had some success in the past catching killers, and I loved that she was so eager to help me yet again.

"I'm afraid we don't have much choice. The chief might believe me, but I have a feeling the residents of April Springs aren't going to be as reasonable."

"Then it's settled. We start digging into this ourselves right now."

"Don't you have to be at work?" I asked. Grace was a supervisor for a popular cosmetics company, but she seemed to spend more time with me than she did at her job.

"That's what the note was for," she said. "My boss called me this morning and told me that she wants a new manager-trainee to take over my responsibilities all week. I'm getting a free vacation."

"You're not worried that she's going to replace you, are you?" I knew just how much of Grace's identity was tied up in what she did for a living, and I didn't know how she'd cope if she ever lost her job.

"No, if Sally passes this test, she's got a management territory in the mountains waiting for her."

"I wouldn't mind that myself," I said. "Don't you want it?"

"All that snow?" Grace asked, shivering a little. "No, thank you." She plucked the note off my windshield and stuck it her purse. "So, who do we talk to first?"

"That's the thing. I'm not really sure. When James came to town, he was like a blank slate. The man never really talked all that much about himself, at least around me. Where did he live before, and what made him want to move here? The problem is that I don't know how to find all of that out."

Grace thought about it, and then said, "I need my computer."

"Is it about work? If you have other things to do, that should come first. I understand."

"It's not for business. They'll do just fine without me, and Sally isn't getting a safety net, either. I want to do some digging online into James Settle's past."

"Do you honestly think there's going to be much there about him?" I asked. Momma and I shared a computer at our cottage, but neither one of us spent a lot of time on it.

"If anything's there, I'll find it. It might take some time, though. Do you want to come back home with me while I dig?"

"Why don't you see what you can come up with and I'll go home and take a shower? I constantly smell like donuts. Big surprise, right?"

"Don't knock it. It must make you a real magnet for men."

I had to laugh. "Jake did say once that he enjoyed it."

"You know, we should bottle that scent ourselves at the company," she said.

"You're not serious, are you?"

"More than you'll ever know. There's an in-house contest for a new fragrance idea, and this might just be a winner."

"How would you ever go about duplicating it?" I asked.

She shrugged. "Fortunately, that part isn't up to me. We leave that to brighter minds than mine." Grace pulled out her telephone, sent a quick text, and then turned back to me. "Done and done," she said.

"Do you think they'll take your idea seriously?"

"There's no doubt in my mind. I'll tell you what I'll do. If I win, I'll share some of the prize money with you. Is it a deal?" she asked as she stuck out her hand.

I took it as I answered, "What have I got to lose? I'll see you at the cottage soon."

"You can count on it."

I followed Grace toward her house — which just so happened to be on the same street as the cottage I shared with my mother — waving good-bye when she pulled into her drive. Just around the bend I saw our small home, and the park right beside it. My donut shop was on the other side of the recreational area, and on beautiful mornings I could walk to work if I didn't mind doing it in the dark. As I parked beside

Momma's car, I marveled at just how tangled the path had been for me to end up there with her again. I'd caught my husband, Max, with another woman from town in a rather compromising position. He had claimed that he was an Actor — yes, with the capital *A* clearly in his voice — and that he had different societal requirements than mere mortals. My divorce attorney had shown him just how wrong he'd been, and I'd bought Donut Hearts with the settlement.

I looked up and found Momma sitting on the front porch. She had a jacket on, and she was clearly enjoying the weather.

"Hey there," I said as I took a seat beside her. "The furnace isn't broken, is it? Please don't tell me that."

"No, I just thought I'd step out here for a while and get a little fresh air," she said. My mother was a tiny slip of a woman, but to underestimate her gigantic spirit was not a mistake anyone ever made twice.

"Did you hear the news?" I asked solemnly.

"About James Settle?"

"Yes, ma'am. It's pretty terrible, isn't it?"

Momma reached over and patted my hand. There was more than just comfort in her touch; I could feel her love for me in it.

"You two were friends, weren't you?"

I nodded. "He was an interesting man to know. How did you find out about what happened to him already?"

"Phillip called me, of course," she said. Momma frowned for a moment as she continued. "He also told me about your conversation in the donut shop."

"Momma, he was just doing his job," I said. "You shouldn't hold it against him."

"I'm doing my best not to, but I must admit that it's odd hearing you defend him."

I shrugged. "Maybe I'm finally coming to grips with the idea of you two being together."

"How big of you," she said with the hint of a smile to take the sting from her gentle sarcasm. "I'm so happy that you're pleased."

I laughed. "That's enough sass from you, young lady."

Momma didn't know what to make of that at first since obviously she was quite a bit older than me. Her laughter was nice to hear when it came, but it died as quickly as it had arrived. "Who do you think might have done it, Suzanne?"

"To tell you the truth, I haven't the slightest clue," I admitted.

Momma paused a moment, and then she looked at me. "But you will before this is all over, won't you?"

"I'm sure I don't know what you're talking about," I said, doing my best to dismiss her question.

"Suzanne Hart, don't try to kid a kidder. I know my daughter too well."

"Did the police chief say anything to you about it?" I was curious to know if he'd already warned her that I'd probably be meddling in the case.

"It may be difficult for you to believe, but Phillip and I have a great deal more to discuss than you when we chat."

"You didn't answer my question, though, did you?" I asked with a slight smile.

She ignored it again. "As lovely as it is out here in nature, why don't we go inside where it's a bit warmer?"

"That sounds great to me. Actually, I've been dying for a shower all day."

"I'm sorry to hear that," Momma said as she pointed toward the driveway. "I have a feeling you're going to have to delay your plans for now."

I looked up and saw that our mayor — and my dear friend — George Morris was approaching. "No problem. I'll be happy to postpone it for George. As a matter of fact, I want to talk to him about this murder."

Momma said, "Suzanne, try not to drag

him into your investigation if you can help it. It was fine when he was just a retired police officer, but he has some serious responsibilities these days."

"Is something going on that I don't know about?" I asked.

"I'm sure there are a great many things that question might envelop, but no, I'm not talking about anything specific. I'm just saying that I would hate to lose our mayor now that we've finally got a good one in office."

"It could have been *you*, you know," I said.

"It's better for everyone that it was George, believe me," she replied. "Good afternoon, Mr. Mayor," she called as he came toward us.

"Please, it's just George," he said with a slight smile.

"Well, then, 'Just George,' " I asked, "would you like something to drink?"

"I wouldn't say no to some sweet tea if you've got any on hand," he said with a smile. His limp, once gone for good — or so I'd thought — was beginning to reappear. Was the stress of his job bringing it out again?

Momma smiled. "As a matter of fact I've got some I made fresh just this morning. I'll be right back with three glasses."

After she was inside, I asked quickly, "George, are you okay?"

"Good as gold," he answered automatically.

"Hey, I want the truth, friend to friend. Your leg's bothering you again, isn't it? Is the mayor's job too tough on you?"

"It's not the job; it's the blasted weather. I'm doing fine, Suzanne, but thanks for asking. I do think we're in for a good soaking rain soon, though." George tugged his ear once, and then he said, "I heard about the blacksmith. I'm really sorry to hear it."

"Me, too," I said.

"You're going to find out who did it yourself, right?" he asked softly.

There was no way I was going to lie to George. "Right."

"Is Grace going to help?"

"As a matter of fact, she's working on it right now," I admitted.

He took that in, and then he asked, "Do you need me for anything?"

Here was the question I'd been hoping he wouldn't ask. "Thanks, but I think that we're good."

George nodded. "I understand, but you know that if I can pull *any* strings for you, all you have to do is ask."

I could swear that he was about to say

something else when Momma came back out onto the porch. She had three glasses of tea on a tray, and handed them out.

I took an easy sip, but George killed half of his in one swig. "That's amazing," he said.

"I'm so glad you like it," Momma replied.

George was about to take another swallow when his phone rang. After a brief and muted conversation, he took another drink, and then handed the glass back to Momma. "Thank you much, ma'am. I'm obliged."

"You're not running off, are you?" she asked him.

"I have to. There's pressing business back at my office."

"I'll walk you to your car," I volunteered.

As we headed for his vehicle, I touched George's sleeve lightly. "Are you sure you're okay?"

"I'm sure, but you keep on worrying about me. I appreciate all of the attention I can get from a pretty girl like you."

As he drove away, I could see him grinning.

I decided to grab that shower while I could. But it was not to be, at least not yet.

When I looked up, I saw that Grace was hurrying up the street toward me on foot with her laptop computer in her hands, and from the expression on her face, she'd clearly hit pay dirt in her search for James Settle's history.

CHAPTER 4

"What did you find out?" I asked Grace the second she got close enough to talk to me. "Did you find anything out about James's background?"

"You are not going to believe this. Let's go inside and I'll show you."

"Come on, don't leave me hanging like that. I want to know now."

"Patience," she said. "It'll be worth the wait; trust me."

As we walked inside, Momma met us at the door. "Hello, Grace," she said, and then turned to me. "Suzanne, I need to go out for an hour or two. Actually, it might even be longer than that. I just don't know yet."

The expression on my mother's face was enough to worry me. "What's wrong? Are you all right?"

"I'm fine," she said. "It's Rita May-weather. She's broken her leg and needs me to pick her up at the hospital. I suspect that once she's in my car, I'll be running errands for her all over town."

I knew that Rita had turned eighty last year, and I felt sorry for her, since she didn't have anyone in her life that could help out if the need arose. "What happened? Did she slip and fall?"

"She surely did. The fool woman was taking salsa dancing lessons and tripped over Hiram Beacon's big feet."

I knew that Hiram was even older than Rita. "Are you serious? They were *dancing*?"

Momma grinned. "Rita's pretty steamed, too. Hiram wanted to be the one who took her home after she got her cast, but she wouldn't let him. They'll work it out soon enough, but for now, I agreed to give her a ride home, and I suspect that it won't end there."

After Momma was gone, Grace and I sat down on the couch and she set her laptop on the coffee table. In just a few seconds, the screen sprang to life, and I saw that Grace had left it on an article about the affluent Pinerush family from a town in central North Carolina bearing the same name.

"Go on. Read it," she said.

"What does this have to do with anything? I thought you were digging into James Settle's life?"

"Believe it or not, I have been," she said.

I looked at the screen and began reading about the wealthy family that founded the town, and all that the next generations had done to add to the Pinerush fortunes. I was nearly to the end when something caught my eye. It was a family photograph from the nineties, and each member was named in the caption below. Off to one side, almost as though he were struggling to get out of the picture, I saw my friend the blacksmith, James Settle. To my dismay, I scanned the names below and saw that he was listed as James Settle Pinerush in the photograph.

"It's James," I said as I sat back, stunned. "He was a *Pinerush*?"

"Oh, yes," Grace said. "And from what I've been able to uncover so far, he was worth a fortune."

"I just can't believe it," I said, remembering James's meager and very rustic cabin on the outskirts of town. I'd visited him once when he'd been sick, bringing him donuts in case he started feeling better, and thinking back on that, I found it hard to imagine him growing up in a life of privilege. "How did he go from this," I asked as I gestured to the article, "to living in April Springs?"

"I'm not exactly sure," Grace said, "but

I've got an address for the family in Pinerush. It's less than sixty minutes away, so we can go there and ask them that ourselves."

"On what pretext?" I asked. "We can't just tell them that we're digging into James's murder."

"We could," Grace said, "but I had another thought. Why don't we tell them the truth; that we were his friends and we both want to offer our condolences to them?"

I nodded. "It's not a bad idea. There's just one problem, though."

"What's that?"

"I don't have any donuts left from today to take them as a gesture of our goodwill."

Grace looked at the house in the photograph and then shrugged. "Somehow I doubt they'll notice if we show up empty-handed. How fast can you get ready?"

"What's wrong with the way I look now?" I asked.

"Suzanne, these folks are loaded, and while I might think that what you've got on is charming, they might not agree. You said yourself you wanted to take a shower anyway, and don't you have one of those dresses you bought from Gabby's shop handy?"

"I have to wear a *dress*?" I asked. Sure,

I'd shopped now and then at Gabby's gently used clothing store, but none of what I'd bought there was part of my standard wardrobe.

"You probably don't *have* to," Grace replied.

"But I should. I know you're right, but I don't have to like it, do I?" I asked with a sliver of a smile. One of the reasons I loved Donut Hearts was because my normal attire of jeans and a T-shirt were always good enough for anything I needed to do, but if dressing up would help us dig into James's murder, then I'd gladly do it.

"I'll see you in twenty minutes," she said. "After all, I need to get dressed up myself."

Grace had a wardrobe that many women would kill for, though I didn't covet it one single bit. In a way, it took the pressure off me. I knew that there was no way I could match her heightened sense of style, so I never even bothered trying. Whatever I wore would just have to be good enough.

I grabbed a quick shower and put on my dress, adding a little makeup as well. I didn't normally get that glammed up even for a date with Jake, and it felt kind of odd doing it now.

I was ready when Grace arrived — mostly because she was a few minutes late — but the time she'd taken had been well spent. She looked like a million dollars, and if I managed to look like a hundred and fifty bucks myself, I'd be happy with the results.

She whistled as she saw me and grinned. "My, my, my; don't you clean up nice, Suzanne?"

"I didn't want to embarrass you by the way I looked," I replied with a smile of my own.

She didn't answer it, though. "Suzanne, you know that you could never do that, don't you?"

"I was just kidding," I said.

"Well, I think you look smashing. So, what do you say? Shall we go?" she asked.

"I'm guessing that we're going to take your company car instead of mine, right?"

Grace's smile returned in force. "We can take whichever vehicle you'd prefer, but I'm not sure how it would look if we drove up to Pinerush manor in your Jeep."

"I am, and I'm pretty sure that it wouldn't be good," I said with a smile. As much as I loved my basic transportation, I knew that it couldn't hold a candle to the car Grace's company provided for her.

As we drove toward Pinerush, I asked, "I've got to admit that I'm still reeling from the news of James's family background. Did you have any idea that he was rich?"

"Not a clue," she acknowledged. "I did a little more digging after I left you, though. That's why I was late, and don't pretend that you didn't notice."

"Two minutes is not late in most folks' eyes," I said.

"Well, I pride myself on my punctuality, but I didn't think you'd mind since it was for a good cause."

"So, what did you discover?"

"It turns out that their original fortune was from coal mining, but it quickly escalated into all kinds of robber-baron behavior by the patriarch of the clan. If you could earn money from the sweat of other people's labors, his family made sure that they had a piece of it, and they thrived over the years by continuing to do it every time they got the opportunity."

"Knowing James, I'm willing to bet that he didn't approve of that."

"That's putting it mildly," Grace said. "I did a Web search on *both* names, James Settle and James Pinerush, and it turned up some interesting things. As a matter of fact, one of the articles I found really shook me up. There was a story buried in a small-town paper around Pinerush that the family clearly couldn't kill. It reported that James tried at one point to give his entire inheritance away, but his family wouldn't let him."

"How could they stop him?" I asked. "It *was* his money, wasn't it?"

"With that much wealth, it's hard to say with any certainty. The thing is, they decided that he didn't know what he was doing when he tried to get rid of it, and they actually claimed that he had literally lost his mind." She shook her head in dismay as she added, "They even had him committed for two days for psychiatric evaluation."

"Wow, that's one rough family. What happened when he got out?"

She shrugged. "I don't know. The article didn't say, and that's the last trace I can find of James Pinerush anywhere online."

"How about as James Settle?"

Grace said, "As far as I can tell he's kept a really low profile on the Web, so I haven't gotten much. I need more time to keep digging."

As she drove on toward the town of Pinerush, I had a sudden thought. "Grace, should we have told Chief Martin about all of this? He might get upset when he finds out what we're doing."

"We've never let that stop us before," Grace said with a smile.

"I know, but things have changed. With

Momma getting so serious with him, I'm trying not to rock the boat at home any more than I have to. Would you mind if I called him?"

She said lightly, "Be my guest. I'll pull off at the next exit and we can turn around."

"Do you think he'll order us to stop?" I asked.

"How could he have any other choice?"

I was sorely tempted to just forget it, but I could see Momma's frown if I did that, so I bit my lip and dialed the chief's cell number.

"Martin," he said quickly as he answered his phone.

"This is Suzanne Hart," I said. "I need to talk to you about something."

"Suzanne, I don't have time right now." Off to one side, he shouted, "Put that down." A second later, he got back on with me. "Sorry, but I have to go," he said, and then hung up on me.

"What did he say?"

"He blew me off," I said as I closed up my phone.

"Does that mean we're going to Pinerush after all?" Grace asked with a smile.

"Hey, we've done our civic duty," I said. "I tried to warn him, but he wouldn't listen to me. My conscience is clear."

"Really? I don't know the last time I could

have said that and actually meant it."

I had to laugh at that. "Yeah, now that I think about it, the same goes for me, too."

It looked like a mansion straight off a movie set as we drove up to the estate where James had grown up. The structure was massive, towering waves of stone after stone, beautifully sculpted grounds, and the beginnings of this spring's garden out front. I half expected a movie star to greet us at the front door, but I wasn't a bit surprised when a man in a suit answered.

"We're here to offer our condolences to the family for their loss," Grace said.

The man barely batted an eye. There was no invitation to enter forthcoming, and I wondered if he planned to leave us out on the front stoop all day. "And you are?" he said with just the right amount of chill in his voice.

"We were both friends of James," I said before Grace could formally introduce us. I didn't like the way the man looked down on us, and I wasn't about to give him any more than I had to. "You have heard the news about him, haven't you?" I had a sudden realization that they might not know what had happened yet. Was I there so soon that I would have to deliver the bad news about James's demise? I surely hoped not.

"We were informed by the police. Please follow me," he said. To my surprise, he led us to the side of the house instead of inside. "If you'll follow me, the gardens are this way."

"Thanks, but we really need to see James's family."

"Mrs. Pinerush is there, collecting her thoughts," he explained.

Okay, I was fine with that. I didn't know what else to say, so I said, "Lead on, then."

Grace looked at me oddly for a second, no doubt wondering where that had come from, but since I didn't know myself, I just smiled softly.

We were led around the side of the house, and then I saw where the real garden was. It was a massive and formal affair that seemed to go on forever, and as we followed the still unidentified man, I had to wonder what the maintenance on the garden alone would cost over the course of a year. Finally, on a bench nestled off to one side, was an older woman who had clearly been crying for some time.

She looked up as we approached, and then told the man in a calm voice, "Stephen, I told you that I was not to be disturbed." Her words had been spoken gently enough, but they'd carried a real bite to them.

"Excuse me, madam, but they say that they were friends of James," he offered in quiet explanation.

She looked startled by the statement, and then turned immediately to us. "Is what Stephen says true?"

"Yes, ma'am," I said. "I'm Suzanne Hart, and this is Grace Gauge. We're both sorry for your loss. Are you James's mother, by any chance?"

"Am I to understand that he didn't speak of me to you? I was his aunt, but since his parents died when he was young, I did my best to raise him. He was always a spirited child, and he did his utmost to frazzle me, but I treated him as one of my very own. Did he never talk about his life here at the manor?"

"Not a word, and I knew him pretty well," I said. It wasn't the nicest thing I could have said, but it was true, and this woman appeared to appreciate frankness in people.

"Why am I not surprised?" She seemed to realize for the first time that we were still standing. Patting the long bench beside her, she said, "Please join me."

Grace and I took seats on either side of her, and once we were settled, she asked, "May I offer you anything? Something to drink, perhaps?"

"Thank you, but no. We're fine."

Once she was assured of that, she turned to the man waiting nearby and said, "Stephen, that will be all. You may go."

He nodded curtly and then walked toward the house.

The second he was out of sight, she said, "Now, we must talk quickly, since we don't have long before Forrest joins us."

"Forrest?" I asked. "Is he your husband?" I thought this woman was in charge, but clearly whoever Forrest was, he was not someone to take lightly.

"In fact, he is my son, but he can be meddlesome and troubling, and I don't want to deal with him at the moment. Now tell me, how exactly did the two of you know James?"

Grace said, "To be honest with you, we just chatted now and then, but Suzanne and he were close friends."

That turned her attention to me. "So, go on, Suzanne. Tell me."

"Well, we got off to a rocky start. We first met having an argument over some old train tracks, and the last time we spoke we were squabbling about the smoke from his fire pit getting into my donut shop, but during all of the time in between, I'm proud to say that we were friends. As a matter of fact, he made me a few things out of iron as presents over the time I knew him."

"What exactly did he make you?" she asked.

"Let's see. I have a beautiful set of bookends he made from railroad tracks, some twisted railroad spikes I use as paperweights, and some skewers he made by hand as well."

She shook her head and said sadly, "What an absolute waste of the man's natural talents. He had such great potential, and in the end he threw it all away to become nothing but a common laborer."

I knew that she was in pain, but I was not about to let that stand. My friend deserved to be defended. "I'm sorry for your loss, but you're wrong there. There was nothing common about James or his work. He was an artist with his anvil and forge. You should see the magnificent things he produced."

"But he most likely had dirt under his fingernails and calluses on his hands when he died." She acted as though it were a great betrayal.

"I'm sure that he did, but he came by them honestly enough. He was a good man," I said. "That was all that counted to me and all of his other friends in April Springs. James made a place for himself among us, and we're going to miss him terribly now that he's gone."

"Then he at least had that much in life," she said with some resignation.

"In my book that's all that really counts," I said. I hadn't come to engage in combat with the grande dame, but I wasn't going to just roll over, either, and let her denigrate what James had accomplished.

She grew pensive as she stared off into the garden for a few moments. "Do the police have any idea who might have killed him, and why? Do either of you?"

I never got the chance to answer her as an overweight man dressed in an elegant suit that had been tailored to fit his bulk came huffing toward us. "Excuse me," he said, nearly out of breath as he approached. "I'm sorry, but my mother is not to be disturbed. We are in mourning."

"We were just offering her our sympathies," I said.

"Thank you for the gesture, but I must ask you to go." He turned to her and offered his hand. "Mother, you'll catch a chill out here. Come inside and warm up."

I was surprised to see this strong woman yield to her son's insistence. As she allowed herself to be led inside, she turned back to us for a moment and said, "Thank you both for coming."

"Yes," Forrest answered. "We *all* appreciate it. Now, if you'll leave us, we'd be even more thankful."

As the man ushered his mother inside, a movement off to one side of the garden caught my eye. Someone had been spying on us from the other side of the hedge that lined the space! I made a little small talk with Grace as I approached the spot I'd seen the movement, and when I got to it, I ordered, "Come out right now or I'll call Forrest!"

There was no action for a few moments, and I began to wonder if it had all been in my imagination when a brawny man dressed in green pants and a matching work shirt stepped out. "No need for that," he said. "The name's Harry Parsons. I saw you approach Mrs. Pinerush following her lapdog Stephen, and I wanted to find out what you two were up to. Is it true what you told her just then?"

"What are you talking about?" I asked.

"Were you really both friends with James?" he asked again, his voice nearly breaking.

"*I* was," I admitted. "As much as he aggravated me at times, he was a valuable friend to me, and I already miss him."

"Then you deserve the truth," he said as

he looked around the grounds. He took another second and glanced at his watch, and then Harry said, "If you want to know anything about James's life at the manor, meet me in town in twenty minutes at the Bell and Whistle café on Oak Street."

Before I could agree or decline, Harry was gone, and when I looked back at the house, I saw that Forrest was watching us closely from the window.

"Let's go," I told Grace. "I don't think we're all that welcome here."

"We're going to meet Harry, though, right?"

"You couldn't stop me if you tried," I said.

When we got to the café in Pinerush, we were early. The diner was well-worn, as though it had seen its brightest lights in the fifties, but it was still comfortable, even though the vinyl in the booths and the linoleum floor were scuffed and faded. A waitress — tall and frail looking, with pale skin and blonde hair — met us at the door and told us to sit anywhere we pleased. We took a booth by the window, and "Lynette," as her name tag read, slid the menus in front of us.

"Start you both off with some sweet tea?" she asked.

"That would be great," I said. "We'll wait to order, though, if that's okay with you. We're waiting for someone."

"Aren't we all, sister?" Lynette asked with a smile as she left to get our tea.

"Are we actually going to eat here?" Grace asked.

"Well, I don't know about you, but lunch didn't hold me, and I'm starving. What's the matter, don't you trust the food?"

She looked around at the other diners, who all appeared to be healthy enough. "Well, none of them are falling over, so we should be okay."

We'd had our teas less than a minute when the door opened and Harry walked through. He scanned the place quickly, offered a few nods of recognition to some of the other patrons, and then joined us at our table.

"Ladies," he said. "Thanks for meeting me." Harry caught Lynette's eye and held up a single finger. She must have known what he wanted, because she nodded in return, a huge smile blooming on her face the instant she saw him.

"Is this your home base?" Grace asked as she'd watched the exchange between them as well.

"It's a matter of habit as much as anything

else," he admitted. "Dad brought me here when I was a kid, and I've kept coming back all these years." As he looked around, he added, "As a matter of fact, Jim tagged along most of the time, too."

"Jim?" I asked. "In all the time I knew James, I never heard him referred to as anything else but his formal name."

"Yeah, well, they used to call me Slick when I was a kid, but I've been Harry for the last ten years, and not many slip up and use my old nickname these days."

"Then you two were close growing up," I said.

Harry looked a little wistful, taking a few moments before answering. "We used to say that we were brothers from different mothers. My father was the landscaper at the manor before me, and we had a place where I still live next to the gardening shed on the grounds."

I must have grimaced slightly at the medieval allusion of serfs working the land for their lords and ladies.

Harry apparently caught it, and he laughed soundly. "I'm not sure what image your imagination just conjured up, but it was a great way to grow up. I had a wonderful little apartment, and all those acres to explore when I wasn't in school. It was just about ideal. For me, anyway," he added as Lynette brought our teas to us.

"Give us a minute before we order anything else, would you?" Harry asked her, and she slipped quietly away. Before she left, though, I caught a glimpse of the way she looked at him when he wasn't aware of it. The woman was clearly in love, but it looked as though Harry didn't have a clue. I wasn't going to bring it up now, but maybe later, if the opportunity presented itself. Jake and Momma both thought that I meddled too much in the lives around me, but how could I just stand idly by while people made mistakes they weren't even aware of?

"Are you implying that James had a rough childhood?" I asked.

Harry took a deep drink of his tea, killing nearly half of it, and the ever vigilant Lynette brought us two cute little plastic pitchers for our refills. Harry smiled at her as she did, and I thought she was going to explode, but she managed to contain it and went back to her station.

After he'd taken another drink, he said, "When we were kids, we both loved living there, but about the time we hit high school, Jim changed."

"What happened?" Grace asked him.

"He wrote a report for our English class

about his family history. We all wrote our own, but some of the things Jim found out were not good. He discovered the source of his family's money and power, and he was never the same after that."

"He took it that hard?" I asked.

Harry nodded solemnly. "By the time we graduated, he'd made up his mind that he never wanted to have anything to do with any of it again, and there was no convincing him otherwise. I talked to him until I was blue in the face, but he wouldn't change his mind. He was going to give his fortune away and move to the mountains. Heck, I was just about ready to follow him, but Dad was determined that I go away for two years to study horticulture after high school, so that was out as far as I was concerned. I couldn't bring myself to go against him, especially since I've always loved the gardens."

"Did James actually leave then?" I asked.

"He did after he got tired of fighting them all. Evidently the money he'd inherited on his eighteenth birthday wasn't really his to give away. It was all tied up in some kind of trust or something like that, and he could get the interest, but not the main chunk of it. The funny thing was he used the money he *did* get from the trust to hire a lawyer to help him do what he wanted to legally."

"What happened?"

Harry shrugged. "It was tied up as tight as he'd feared."

"What did he do when he found out he couldn't touch it?" I asked.

"He got out of here as fast as he could go. He'd been accepted at Stanford on a full academic scholarship, so he left for California and never looked back. At least not right away." He refilled his tea glass with one of the pitchers, and then asked, "Would you two mind if I eat while we talk? I only have so much time before I have to get back."

"That sounds good," I said. "If you let it be our treat. After all, we're the ones benefiting from this."

"Don't mind if I do," Harry said with a reckless smile.

"Anything you'd recommend? We're hungry, too."

Harry stared at us for a few seconds, and then he asked, "Do you like meat loaf and mashed potatoes? If you do, don't order it here. It's the worst thing on the menu. I don't know why Kenny even insists on serving it."

I had to laugh. "Okay, we'll cross that one off our list. What are you going to have?"

"I always get the hamburger steak with grilled peppers and onions, green beans, and fries. You can believe me when I say that it's much better than it sounds."

"I don't know; it sounds good to me," I said, and he motioned to Lynette. Grace agreed to try it, and Lynette took our orders. Before we could return to our conversation, she came back with three heaping plates of food.

"That was fast," Grace said.

"It's today's special, so Kenny keeps a lot of it back there," Harry said.

As promised, it was indeed delicious. The hamburger steak was cooked to a perfect medium-well, and the onions and peppers were wonderful. The beans were clearly homegrown and canned, and the fries didn't even need catsup they were so good. As hard as it was to ignore the food and focus on our guest, I did my best, sneaking bites as I asked Harry more about James.

Finishing a French fry, I asked, "When did he come back for the last time?"

Harry thought about it a second, and then told us. It was right before he'd first showed up in April Springs asking about the old railroad tracks near Donut Hearts. Had he come straight from the manor to join our little community?

"That's about when he moved to our town," I said.

Harry nodded. "Something bad happened here, and he wasn't about to stay. Besides, he never *was* cut out for life around here. It doesn't surprise me one bit that he ended up there." With a wistful tone in his voice, Harry said, "He called me a few times after he left, but he was actually afraid that the phones were bugged on the estate. I told him my cell phone was clean, but he wouldn't risk it. We were planning on going fishing next summer, but that's not going to happen now."

"We know what really happened. When exactly was he locked up?" I asked as delicately as I could.

Harry's expression hardened, and I saw his hands go white as he clenched them. "Forrest is going to pay for that someday. He thinks it's over, but he's wrong."

From the sound of his words, the threat wasn't idle, and I was happy not to be Forrest. "He had it done himself?"

"He surely did. Mrs. Pinerush was too sick to fight him on it, and Forrest waited until she didn't have the strength to oppose him. You saw it for yourselves a little bit ago. She's a different woman when he's around, like he's got some kind of hold over her. The woman's afraid of her own son. Imagine that, would you? I don't remember much of my own mother — she died when I was just a kid — but I never would have treated her like that." He shook himself, as if trying to wipe all of the bad memories away, and then took another bite of his lunch.

"What set it off?" Grace asked.

"James came back to the manor with a piece of paper renouncing his fortune once and for all, but all he got for his trouble was two nights in the loony bin. Pardon me, the state mental facility, that's the proper name for it these days. They couldn't keep him, but it was enough to make Jim realize that he wasn't ever going to be able to give away his fortune, so he just left it with them. He told them that he didn't want to have anything to do with any of them or their money. Jim even signed over his interest payments to a charity, the Poor Children Among Us. If he couldn't do any good with the bulk of his money, he was determined to do something with the interest to try to redeem his family's name and honor."

"I don't understand that part of it," I said. "What business is it of anyone else's what he did with his inheritance?"

Harry finished his meal and pushed the plate away as he explained, "I don't get it, either, not completely, but supposedly there's some kind of iron-clad clause that keeps it in the family forever. If Jim ever did manage to get rid of his share, everyone else would lose theirs, too. The old man who had it drawn up was a big believer in family, even though you couldn't tell it by the way his people act now."

A sudden and chilling thought struck me. "Do you have any idea what happens to his share now that he's gone? Is there any way you can find out?"

"I already know," Harry said. "When Mr. Pinerush's sister passed away a few years ago, they were all whispering about it. It all goes back into the family trust, and with Jim gone, that means that a third of it is now Mrs. Pinerush's money, a third belongs to Forrest, and the last third goes to another one of Jim's cousins."

"Do you know who that cousin might be?" I asked. "Was it a man or a woman?"

"It's a man, but that's about all I know about him. He was Mr. Pinerush's sister's son, and they had a falling-out a long time ago when the kid was just a baby. I guess they'll have to track him down and tell him that he's even richer now than he was before."

"So, he wouldn't be a Pinerush by name, would he?" Grace asked.

"No. I'm sorry, but I don't know his name, first or last." He leaned in for a moment and added softly, "If there's anything I can do to help you find Jim's killer, you both should know that you can count on me."

"What makes you think we're searching for the murderer?" I asked. Were Grace and I that obvious?

Harry laughed. "I've read enough books to realize that you don't ask the kind of questions you've been asking unless you're hunting down bad guys. Don't worry; you can trust me."

I looked at Grace, who nodded slightly, and then I said, "It's true. We're going to find his killer if we can."

"Thanks for coming clean with me. You won't regret it." Harry gave us his cell number, and I gave him mine in return.

"Even if you don't need my help, do me a favor, would you?" Harry asked as he stood.

"If we can," I said.

"No matter what happens, call me and tell me if you ever find out what really happened to Jim, would you? It might not help me sleep at night, but it's worth a shot. We might not have been close at the end, but he was my brother in all the ways that ever mattered, and I won't be able to let this go until I know his killer is caught."

"We will," I promised.

As he walked out of the diner, I saw him say something to Lynette, and then leave.

"What do you make of all of that?" Grace asked me.

"It's almost too much to take in all at once, isn't it? Why don't we head back to April Springs? We can discuss it along the way, and maybe even figure out what we should do next."

"That's a deal," Grace said as she grabbed the check.

"I'll split it with you," I said.

"Thanks, but I just got a nice bonus, so I'll pick this one up and you can get the next one."

I knew better than to try to argue with her. "Thanks."

It turned out that neither one of us had to pay, though. When Grace approached Lynette with the bill, she shook her head. "Thanks for trying, but your bill is taken care of. Harry already got it."

"That's not fair. He promised us that *we* could pay," I said.

She just laughed. "You are beating your head against the wall if you think that will ever happen. It's best just to accept his kindness and move on."

"At least thank him for us," Grace said as she put her money away.

"That I can do. You ladies have a nice day."

"You, too," I said.

As we got into Grace's car and headed back to familiar territory, I couldn't help thinking that Harry knew more about James's recent past than he was letting on. Even with that cautionary feeling, I still believed that we could trust him.

I just hoped that I was right.

CHEESY FRITTER BALLS

When I first saw a variant of this recipe for fried rounds I wasn't at all sure about it, but after I added and subtracted some of the listed ingredients and converted the recipe into one for dropped fritters, these tasty treats have found a good home with me and my family.

Ingredients

Mixed
- 1 egg, lightly beaten
- 1 cup cottage cheese, drained
- 2 tablespoons sugar, white granulated
- 1/4 cup half-and-half

Sifted
- 3/4 cup flour, unbleached all-purpose
- 2 teaspoons baking powder
- 1 teaspoon nutmeg
- Dash of salt

- Canola oil for frying (the amount depends on your pot or fryer)

Instructions

In one bowl, beat the cottage cheese, half-and-half, and the egg together. In a separate bowl, sift together the flour, baking powder, nutmeg, and salt.

Add the dry ingredients to the wet, mixing well until you have a smooth consistency.

Drop bits of dough using a small-sized cookie scoop (the size of your thumb, approximately). Fry in hot canola oil (360 to 370 degrees F) 1 1/2 to 2 minutes, turning halfway through.

Yield: 10–12 fritters

CHAPTER 5

"Suzanne, maybe we should move our investigation to Pinerush," Grace said as she started to head home.

"Do you think there's a chance we'll get anything out of them that we didn't learn today?" I asked her. "James was killed in the park across from my shop, but I'm still not convinced that the murderer could be somebody from our town."

She quickly glanced at me and then asked, "You don't have any idea how much we're talking about here, do you?"

"A couple of million, I guess."

"More like a hundred million plus," she replied.

I couldn't help whistling softly at the news. "Maybe you're right. That's a *lot* of money, and that means a pretty strong motive, but I still think we'll have more luck digging into James's life in April Springs. After all, he wasn't a threat to anybody in

Pinerush. I've got the feeling that the stay in the mental ward was enough to make him want to do his best to forget about ever trying to give away his fortune again."

"Why do you say that?"

"Think about it. Instead of getting a new attorney to keep fighting them after he was released, James ran away to April Springs and most likely did his best to put all of that behind him. I never had any idea that he came from money, and I knew him just about better than anyone else in town. Those three folks who inherited already had more money than they could ever know what to do with. There was no reason to kill him and risk going to jail."

"That's not how it works sometimes. With some folks, the more they have, the more they want. I still think that we should keep them all in mind as suspects," Grace said.

"Don't get me wrong; I agree, but I think it would be a mistake to put all of our focus on the three of them. Shoot, we don't even know the name of one of them, unless you can track it down on the Internet. Just for now, let's forget about focusing on the money. Who do we know in April Springs who might have wanted to see James dead?"

Grace nodded slightly. "I believe that his new apprentice might have had a grudge.

James was riding him pretty hard, from what I've heard."

"Where'd you hear that?" I asked.

"Suzanne, I hear things," she said with a slight grin.

"Well, I don't care what you heard. Murphy Armstrong is no killer," I said. "And he wasn't exactly an apprentice, either. James told me that the man worked for him two Saturdays a month learning some blacksmithing basics. That was it."

"Maybe so, but he wasn't exactly easy on him."

"I don't have the least bit of trouble believing that. James always demanded perfection from himself *and* everybody around him," I replied. "If that was all it took, it would make Rebecca Link more of a suspect than Murphy."

"Were they even still dating?" Grace asked. "I knew that James had seen her a while back — and pretty seriously, too — but I thought they'd ended it."

"They did, but she wanted to get back together," I told her.

"What did James think about it?"

"He ran hot and cold about the idea until recently."

"What changed?"

"He wouldn't say, but from the grin he

sported lately, it wouldn't surprise me to hear that he met someone else."

"You don't know who it might have been, though, right?"

"Right. All I'm sure of is that it wasn't Rebecca."

"Then she goes on our list," Grace said. "Agreed?"

"Yes, it makes sense." I reached over and grabbed a small embossed notebook Grace always kept beside her. "Do you mind if I use this for a minute?"

"Go right ahead. I have a dozen more just like it at home."

"You hoarder, you," I said with a smile as I opened it and took out the pencil inside.

"Hey, I find something I like and I stick with it."

"That's why we're still friends, right?"

"Yeah, *that*'s it," she said.

I opened the notebook to a blank page and wrote down the names: Mrs. Pinerush, Forrest Pinerush, Mystery Cousin, Murphy Armstrong, and Rebecca Link. "We already have five names on our list. Who knew that many people might want to see harm come to James?"

"I imagine that we both could come up with a list like that for each one of us if we put our minds to it."

"Me maybe, but everybody knows that you're an angel," I said with a smile.

"You'd be surprised. Then again, you know me better than anyone else, so you probably realize that was a load of hooey the second you said it. I wonder if there's anyone else we need to add to this?"

"The only way we can find out is to keep digging," I said. "I can miss a little sleep."

"I'm game if you are. Where should we go now?"

I thought about it, and then suggested, "How about paying a visit to James's cabin?"

"Don't you think Chief Martin has already been there?" Grace asked.

"I'm counting on it. He can catch all of the obvious clues, but I can't imagine that he got everything there is to learn out of it."

"Then let's do it," Grace said.

By the time we got to James Settle's place in the woods, darkness was just beginning to touch the sky. It was a rustic cabin, barely bigger than twelve feet by sixteen. The siding was weathered board and batten, overlapping sections that had all weathered into a uniform pleasing gray. I loved it, but it was a far cry from the place Grace and I had visited earlier. How could James have possibly gone from living in a place as elegant as the manor to a place as rustic as this? Then again, I was certain that this cabin had suited him better than the mansion ever had.

"There's just one problem. We don't have a key, Suzanne," Grace said as we walked up onto the porch. I was relieved to see that there was no police tape over the door. Though I knew the murder had happened in town, there was still no assurance that Chief Martin would release James's place so quickly.

"When I brought James donuts once when he was sick, he told me where to find the key, so unless someone's taken it, it shouldn't be a problem." I looked for the loose board just off the door James had told me about, and after a few false starts, I found it. As it swung aside, I saw the key hanging there. The lock was massive, and clearly hand-forged, as were the door's large hinges. No doubt James had made them himself.

I slid the key in, and the door opened easily.

"Well, at least it won't be hard to search," Grace said as soon as we walked inside the tight quarters. "It's kind of small, isn't it?"

"You *could* think of it as cozy," I countered.

"We're not selling it as real estate. Let's call it what it is," Grace said with a smile. As she searched the wall for a switch, I said, "Don't bother. James used kerosene lamps for his lighting at night."

"You've got to be kidding me," Grace answered. She loved her luxuries, and her idea of roughing it was not having room service at a fine hotel.

I lit the kerosene lamp so we wouldn't be caught by the pending darkness, and it was enough to throw a soft yellow glow into the room. A massive fireplace anchored one end, and the other had a simple bed and dresser. Between them, there was a kitchen on one side and a small table and two chairs on the other. There was a sofa and a small desk near the fireplace, and bookcases were present in just about every other open spot.

"Where's the bathroom?" she asked.

I pointed outside to the outhouse, and her dismay blossomed.

"Suzanne, this is like some kind of twisted time machine."

"I never said that James wasn't a bit of an odd bird," I answered. "He believed this cabin matched his attitude, and who are we to dispute it? I'll take the desk and you search the rest of the place."

"That shouldn't take either one of us very

long," she said.

I opened the desk drawers and started examining the papers inside. There was a small bound notebook inside one, and I opened it and scanned it quickly. It was part "to do" list, part reminder, and part journal. I wondered if it might lead to any insights into James's life — and more importantly, who might want to kill him. I couldn't easily decipher his chicken-scratch handwriting in the flickering yellow light, so without conscious thought, I tucked it into my purse. There would be time to examine it later, but for right now, I needed to finish searching his desk. On top of the stack of papers in the second drawer, I found a greeting card with a large red heart on the front, broken once, but now secured again with tape. Inside, it said,

James, You NEED to FORGIVE me. I CAN'T go on like this. I MEAN IT.

Rebecca's name was scrawled at the bottom.

"Grace, you've got to see this."

I handed her the card and watched her expression as she read it. "Wow, did she just threaten him at the same time that she was asking for a reconciliation? The girl's a little volatile, wouldn't you say?" Grace put it down and took a quick photo of it with her phone.

"She might think she's just being passionate, but if you ask me, I believe she's just a little bit crazy. Wow, James picked a real winner there, didn't he?"

"I can see why he wanted to get away from her," she said as she looked past the card into the open drawer.

Grace plucked something out of it, and I protested, "Hey, that's my job."

"You can read it when I'm finished," she said with a smile.

"At least let me read it over your shoulder."

"Fine," she said, and we both moved closer to the light. This was written in thick pencil on a plain sheet of notebook paper, and the force of some of the writing had been so intense that the paper was actually torn in a few places.

James, enough is enough. I'm not your whipping boy. Back off, or you'll regret it.

"Wow, James seemed to bring out the emotions in people, didn't he?" she said as she got a snapshot of that as well.

"I'll say," Suzanne answered. "I wonder why the police chief didn't take these when they searched the place?"

The door must have opened while we'd

been reading, because I hadn't heard a thing. It was a testament to James's skill in making hinges that moved so effortlessly as well as the engrossing reading.

"He didn't take them because he hasn't seen them yet," Chief Martin said with a heavy tone in his voice. "What are you two doing in here? You're both directly interfering with an active police investigation. You realize that, don't you?"

"We thought you'd already come and gone," I admitted.

"So, that gives you the right to just break in here? Is that what you're saying?"

"I knew about the key," I explained, "and James expressly invited me to use it whenever I wanted."

"I suppose you have proof of that?" he asked.

"No, but think about it. I knew where the key *was,* didn't I?"

"Suzanne, you both need to leave, and I mean right now." There was no room for play in his voice, and I knew that he was serious.

"We'll be glad to," I said. "Be sure to check out the card and the letter on top of the desk, though."

"I'll conduct my own investigation, thank you very much."

As we were leaving, he called out to me, "Is this why you called me earlier? Were you actually asking for my permission? And why are you both so dressed up? I know Jake's out of town, so why are you wearing a dress, Suzanne?"

"Hey, a girl can choose to look pretty whenever she wants to without a man having to be involved in the decision," I said. I was trying to deflect his original question, seeing the kind of mood he was in at the moment. I'd considered going ahead and telling him the truth about why I'd called him, but I wasn't sure how much information I should volunteer. The journal in my purse felt red-hot and I knew instantly that I should turn it over to him, but if I did that, we might miss a golden opportunity to investigate a little more. I didn't plan to keep it forever anyway; I was just going to search through it tonight and mail it to the chief tomorrow anonymously. Maybe I was playing a little fast and loose with the law, but there was no way that my curiosity would let me turn it over before I had a chance to do more than just glance at it.

Grace and I were almost outside when he asked, "What was that telephone call about, then? Why were you calling me?"

I didn't have any choice now. As I turned

to face him, I said, "I shouldn't have to explain it to you, Chief. You already contacted James's next of kin."

He was clearly puzzled by my response. "True. He had a contact card in his wallet with a phone number, and I had Lincoln call it and give them the bad news," he admitted. "They haven't come to identify the body yet, though."

"And that's all that you know?" I asked. Wow, Grace's Internet search had been more effective than the April Springs police investigation.

I knew that he wasn't going to like what I was about to tell him, but I had to share the information nonetheless. "We were going to Pinerush, and I wanted to touch base with you first."

"What were you doing there, and why would you need my approval?"

It was time to come clean with all that Grace and I had discovered. Well, most of it anyway. "It turns out that James Settle wasn't his real name. At least not all of it."

The chief looked surprised by the statement. "Do you mean that it was an alias?"

"Sort of. His full name was James Settle Pinerush, so we went to see his family so that we could pay our respects. It's just the polite thing to do," I added.

As I'd figured, Chief Martin didn't like that one little bit. "Admit it. You were both snooping. You two are digging into this mess, aren't you?"

"Like I said, we went to Pinerush to offer our condolences," I repeated.

"And nothing else?" he asked as he studied us both.

"We might have asked a few questions about James's life when he lived there."

The police chief was clearly unhappy with that. "What did they say?"

"It sounded like a nightmare, to be honest with you. His aunt and her son had him committed to a mental institution when he tried to give his share of their fortune away, and the second he got himself free, he came here to live in April Springs."

"They told you all of that?" The chief of police looked amazed by what we'd discovered so far.

"We might have also picked up a few things off the Internet," I said casually, holding Harry's name back unless I absolutely had to rat him out. He'd most likely lose his job if the Pinerushes found out that he'd talked to us, and I couldn't have that on my conscience.

"Let me guess. They were after his money

themselves. How much are we talking about?"

When I told him, he just shook his head. "We all know that people have been killed for a lot less than that."

"True, but they can't be your only suspects. If they left James alone, he wouldn't have bothered them again. From what we heard, being locked up was enough to cure him of his desire to be a philanthropist for a lifetime. He came here for a fresh start. The money didn't interest him one bit, either keeping it or giving it all away."

"How can you say that with any certainty?"

"Look around you, Chief. Does this strike you as a place a man worth many millions would live? He didn't even keep the interest after his stay at the hospital ward. Every bit of it went to the Poor Children Among Us. It pays to feed poor kids around here instead of off somewhere in the world."

"I know. I manage to give them some myself every now and then."

It was another side of Chief Martin's heart, which Momma claimed was strong and true. I rarely saw many glimpses of it myself, but this was a sure sign that he at least had a sense of what was right. It was a point for him that I tallied a little reluctantly.

Slowly but surely, I was warming up to the man, and I still wasn't sure how I felt about the change in our status. "So, if he cared anything about money, I doubt he would have lived here."

The chief nodded. "I can see that, but I still can't rule them out, no matter what the two of you might think." He paused, and then asked, "You both are going to keep at this, aren't you?"

"We'll do our utmost not to interfere with your investigation, but folks around town are already whispering that I might have been involved in his murder despite your endorsement earlier. I really don't have much choice."

"You could leave it all in my hands and trust me," he said with a slight smile.

"You're right; I could do that," I answered, doing my best to keep a straight face.

"But you're not, are you?"

"Not so much," I replied.

"Just don't do anything that might embarrass your mother, or make *me* embarrass her."

There was a bit of a sting to his words, though he hadn't changed his tone or demeanor. My mother was a powerful woman in April Springs, and I would have never knowingly done anything to cause her embarrassment. Then again, I'd managed a few times in the past despite my good intentions, so it wasn't as though the chief didn't have a point.

"I'll do the best I can," I said.

He nodded, and as he turned to go back inside, I grabbed Grace and got out of there. If we hung around the cabin much longer, I was sure we'd get instructions very soon not to talk to Rebecca and Murphy.

"What's the rush?" Grace asked as we neared her car.

"We need to find our two other suspects before the chief tracks them down himself," I said.

Grace nodded, and it was clear that she didn't have any problems with that strategy. "I'm not sure where Murphy is, but Rebecca is bound to be at work. She's been pulling double shifts at the Happy Stop convenience store out on the highway for months."

"That sounds good. Grace, do you happen to have a small flashlight in your pocket that I could use while you drive?"

"Sure, there's one in my purse. Help yourself. What are you going to look at?"

I pulled the journal out of my purse and held it up. "I know I should have given this to Chief Martin, and I will the first thing tomorrow, but I had to see what it said for myself first."

"You took that from James's desk?" she asked incredulously.

"I know. I shouldn't have done it. Are you disappointed in me?"

"Are you kidding? I couldn't be any prouder of you than I am right now. Hang on a second." She pulled her car off into the church parking lot and turned on the lights in the car. "Now we can both read it together."

I opened the book and started scanning the pages. At first it didn't look like much, filled with entries about new designs and sketches, a grocery list or two, and even the addresses of some of his clients.

"It's not much, is it?" Grace asked, clearly disappointed by my find.

"What a letdown. Now I really regret not giving it to the chief," I said.

"You keep looking, and I'll drive to Happy Stop."

As she drove, I flipped through the pages quickly. What I'd assumed at first glance was a journal entry was actually something detailing a new technique for welding iron. It looked to be a complete bust. I was about to put it away when something on the very last page caught my eye.

It was a phone number, but that wasn't the most surprising part.

What nearly threw me for a loop was the name scrawled under it.

It was Trish Granger, my dear friend who ran the Boxcar Grill. Now, why in the world would James have her number? Was she the new woman in his life that I suspected? It would explain why she'd reacted so badly to the news of his murder.

I pulled out my phone and Grace asked, "Who are you calling?"

"Nobody," I said as I started punching buttons to call up my personal contact list.

"Sorry to doubt you, but it looks suspiciously like that's exactly what you're doing."

"Hang on a second and I'll explain," I said. I got to Trish's info, and sure enough, below the number for the diner was her cell phone number. Almost nobody had that one because Trish hated people calling her when she was off. She'd told me once just three people had it, and that I should be honored that I was one of them.

It looked like now there were four, though.

"Trish's number is in James's book."

"For the diner? That doesn't surprise me. He probably ordered a lot of takeout food. You saw that kitchen of his."

"No, you don't understand; it's her personal number. When I spoke with her earlier today, she was really upset. I thought it was because there was a murder so close to the diner, but now I'm starting to think that it's something a lot more than that."

Grace whistled softly. "That's not good. What are you going to do?"

"We obviously need to talk to her, but there are a few more pressing conversations we need to have first."

"I mean about the number. Are you going to just leave it in there, or are you going to tear it out of the book?"

I stared down at the book, wishing that I'd never taken it. "As much as I want to rip out the page, I can't. It's just not right destroying something that might be evidence."

"Do you actually think that she might have done it?" Grace asked, having a hard time believing it herself.

"Of course not, but that doesn't mean I can tamper with this journal. I'm sure she'll be cleared, but she has to go through the process first."

Grace nodded, and then asked casually, "What would you have done if it had been my telephone number written there?"

"I'd have a lot of questions for you, that's

for sure," I said, trying to blow it off.

"Seriously," Grace said.

I thought about it. "Grace, I would still leave it there for the police. Before you get upset, you should know that I'd expect you to do the exact same thing if it were my name and number there instead. In nine out of ten cases, we both know that the cover-up is worse than the crime. Not to say that I think that any one of us would ever kill someone, but it's better to bring this out in the open sooner rather than later."

"That makes sense," Grace said. "Still, it's pretty pragmatic of you to feel that way."

"We've both been around these investigations enough to realize that the truth has a way of getting loose, and the harder you try to hide it, the more it fights to get free."

Just to be certain, I scanned each page of the journal one more time, but there was nothing else of interest there. When I looked up, I saw that we were nearing the police department. "Pull in," I told Grace.

"Why, are you going to confess something?" she asked with a smile.

As I wiped the book with my T-shirt as best I could, I explained, "We're going to drop this off in the mailbox so it can get into the right hands."

"And you don't think the chief will suspect that it was us?"

"Oh, I'm betting he'll be sure of it, but I doubt that he'll say anything to us about it."

Grace raised an eyebrow as she asked, "Why would you possibly think that?"

"He doesn't want to cause any more trouble with Momma than he has to. They're already on edge with each other about me, and I've got a feeling the chief will let this one slide to insure a little harmony with my mother."

"Suzanne Hart, are you using your personal status for your own gain?"

"You bet I am," I answered with a smile. "It's about time I could use it somehow for something besides getting into trouble. Hang on, I'll be right back."

I was walking to the mailbox and ready to slip the journal inside when someone called my name from the shadows and nearly gave me a heart attack in the process.

"Suzanne, what are you up to now?"

There was no way I was getting away with this.

My heart finally stopped racing when I saw Officer Grant step out of the darkness and walk toward me.

"What are you doing out lurking in the dark like that?" I asked.

"I wasn't lurking," he said with a smile I could see from the streetlight's illumination. "I'm on the desk again, and this is my ten-minute break. I came outside because I wanted to see what fresh air was like again."

"Wow, he really doesn't like you, does he?"

"The chief has his reasons for everything he does," Grant said, and I admired him for his ability to keep his true feelings to himself. At least I hoped he didn't actually believe what he was saying. Hiding the way I really felt about people was a skill I hadn't even come close to mastering yet.

"I asked you a question," he repeated a little more firmly. "What's going on, and why are you wearing a dress?"

"Why is everyone making such a fuss about it? It's not like it never happens."

"It's rare enough to note," he said. "But that doesn't explain anything, does it?"

"I found something, and I thought the chief might like to see it," I said as I held the journal up in the air.

"What is it?" he asked.

As I started to hand it over, I explained, "This belonged to James Settle. I found it earlier, and I thought the chief should see it."

"Where did you come across it?" he asked, being very careful not to touch it.

"In his cabin just before Chief Martin got there," I admitted. I wasn't going to lie to my friend. "Only I'd appreciate if you'd tell him that it was dropped off here anonymously."

He shook his head as he put his hands in his pockets. "I'm sorry, but I won't lie to my boss for you."

"Does that mean that you don't want it?" I asked incredulously.

"Not in my hands. Now if you'll excuse me, I need to get back to my desk."

As he started to turn back, he said, "I usually check the mailbox on my next break. If I should happen to find something in there, I'd have no real way of knowing how it got there, now would I?"

After Officer Grant was back inside, I smiled as I dropped the journal into the mailbox. He'd given me an out, and I'd taken it gladly.

As I got back into the car, Grace said, "For a second there, I thought I was going to have to use our emergency bail money to get you out of jail."

"Do you really have a fund earmarked just for that?"

"You'd better believe it. I've been saving

since we first started digging into murders. One of these days it's going to come in really handy."

"Just not today, gladly." I recounted my exchange with Officer Grant, and she laughed when she heard his solution. "The man's clever, isn't he?"

A thought suddenly occurred to me. Grace had had some truly horrid luck in the past in her love life. Maybe she'd been going after the wrong kind of men. "And nice looking, too."

"Suzanne, I thought you were happy with Jake."

"I am," I said quickly. "But you're available. You could do a lot worse than him."

"Date a cop? I don't know about that."

I laughed. "Don't knock it until you try it. If you need a couple of testimonials, Momma and I would be happy to provide them."

"I didn't mean anything by what I just said," she added quickly.

"I know that. I'm just saying, he's a good guy in my book, and there isn't an overabundance of those roaming the streets these days."

"Or any days," she replied.

I thought about pushing a little harder, but knowing Grace, that was the worst thing

I could do. I'd planted the seed, and now it was time to step back and see if it sprouted. I honestly believed that Grace deserved another chance at love.

CHAPTER 6

As Grace pulled up to the convenience store parking lot, I glanced at my watch. It was getting late, at least for me, but this was too important to just pass up. We walked inside, ready to question Rebecca about her relationship with James and her alibi, but there was an older heavyset man behind the register instead.

"Is Rebecca here?" I asked.

He shook his head. "No, she called in sick. There was a death in the family."

I nodded, and Grace and I left the store. "It looks like she's taking it hard."

"You read the card, too," Grace said. "Neither one of us should be surprised. So, should we go looking for Murphy now?"

"Okay," I said, stifling a yawn.

Grace shook her head. "Suzanne, I can be a real dope sometimes. You need to go home and get some sleep."

"It's okay," I insisted.

"No it's not. I don't want to be the one who's responsible if you put cherry filling in the lemon-filled donuts tomorrow. I've got some errands to run in the morning, but I'll be at the shop at eleven-thirty, okay? We can pick up where we left off."

"That sounds great, if you're sure you don't mind," I said. I was beat, even though the hour was early for just about anyone else. To be fair, though, they didn't have to get up when I did, either.

She dropped me off at my Jeep, and I followed her home. As Grace turned into her driveway, I beeped my horn once and headed on to the cottage Momma and I shared. I was looking forward to a quick conversation on the phone with Jake, and then an abbreviated night's sleep.

I had the perfect plan, but I never got to use it.

Momma was standing by the front door, and from the expression on her face, we were about to have a conversation that I was nearly positive I wasn't going to enjoy.

"Young lady, what exactly have you been up to this evening?" she asked the second my foot hit the first step.

"You're going to have to be little more specific than that, Momma. Otherwise, I wouldn't even know where to start."

She didn't crack a smile at that, a bad sign. "I just spoke with Phillip on the telephone. What were you thinking?"

"Was he honestly *that* upset Grace and I were at James's cabin? I didn't think he had a huge problem with it at the time."

Momma frowned as she somehow managed to look down on me, a neat trick since we were both on the porch and I was a good half a foot taller than she was. "I'm talking about the journal, Suzanne."

So Officer Grant had ratted me out after all. He was going to get a stale donut the next time he came into the shop. "He actually called you about that?"

"What would you rather have had him do, arrest you?"

"Momma, I gave it right back," I protested.

"Suzanne Hart, I will not tolerate this kind of behavior. You stepped over the line, and you need to make this right with Phillip, and I mean right now. I will not have you stealing evidence in a murder investigation, not to mention interfering with my relationship with your actions, do you understand?"

"James was my friend. I have a right to find out what happened to him, especially after the way we left things. Momma, I yelled at him, and the next thing I heard about him, he was dead. There's no way that I can make it right with him now, but I have to do everything in my power to try to find his killer."

Her voice softened, and she stroked my cheek gently for a moment, something she'd done when I'd been upset as a little girl. It still managed to have a calming influence on me. "I understand all of that, and I know that you're in some pain. That still doesn't change the fact that you were wrong this evening."

I considered her words for a few moments, and then I nodded in agreement. "You're right. I was wrong."

Momma looked hard into my eyes. "Are you just trying to placate me?"

"No, ma'am." I grabbed my cell phone and dialed the chief's number.

He picked up on the first ring and barked out, "Martin."

"Chief, this is Suzanne. I'm sorry I didn't give you the journal right away. I guess I kind of panicked when you walked into the cabin, so I was afraid to tell you that I had it, but that's no excuse. I was wrong to do it, and I sincerely apologize."

"Did you tamper with it in any way?"

Boy, was I glad that I'd left Trish's number right where I'd found it. "No, sir. I give you my word."

There was a long pause on his end of the line, and then he finally said, "That's good enough for me, then. Just promise me one thing. If you find anything else, let me know about it right away, okay? Slipping it into the mailbox was a bad way to handle it. The second I pulled it out of the box I knew what you must have done."

So then Officer Grant hadn't betrayed me after all. That was good to know, and made me feel a little better about things. And then the ramifications of the chief's words hit me. "Does that mean that you approve of my digging?"

"Hang on a second. I never said anything like that, but I know you too well to believe you're going to just drop this on your own unless I lock you up. Just don't get in my way, or make my life any harder than it already is, okay?"

"Is that just on the professional front, or elsewhere, too?"

"Consider it a blanket request," he said. There was another pause, and he added the next bit so softy I nearly missed it. "If it's any consolation, I just found out that James died almost instantly. The skewer pierced his heart from the front, and he was most likely dead before he hit the ground. I *am* sorry about your loss. I know that the two of you were close."

"Thank you for that," I said, and then hung up.

"There, was that so bad?" Momma asked me.

"It wasn't good," I said, "but you were right. It had to be done." The chief hadn't mentioned Trish's name, so I knew that he hadn't found it yet.

"What's the occasion?" Momma asked. "You look lovely tonight."

"Grace and I decided to get dressed up for a change," I said, "but don't get used to it. I'm going to change in just a second back into jeans."

"I'm glad I got to see it, then."

As tired as I was, I couldn't go to sleep yet. "Momma, after I put on some jeans and a T-shirt, I have to go out for a little while. I'm not all that hungry, since I had a really late lunch. Do you mind?"

"We're having leftovers, so you can eat whenever you'd like. You aren't digging into James's death more after that telephone call, are you?"

"When I saw Trish this afternoon, she was upset. I'm worried about her, so I thought I'd go by her place to check on her." It was tied into the case in a few ways, both from

130

her earlier reaction and also from her telephone number showing up in James's journal, but I didn't have to add that to my explanation. The main purpose *was* to see how my friend was doing.

"You're a good friend," she said. "Go on."

I felt bad about misleading her even a little, but if I told Momma *all* of the reasons I wanted to see my friend, I was afraid it would just start another round of squabbles, and I wasn't in the mood for that right now. I left the house, got into my Jeep, and drove straight to Trish's house by the lake. I thought about calling her first to let her know that I was on my way, but if I did that, I knew that there was a good chance she wouldn't see me. Better to show up and make her turn me away in person, if she thought she could manage to do that. I had to see just how involved Trish was in this murder, and preferably before Chief Martin showed up on her doorstep.

It wasn't a very long drive, but it might as well have been in a different county. Trish had inherited a place on the lake from her grandfather. It was nothing grand — just barely more than a cottage — but it was right on the water, and as much as I loved the park just outside my bedroom window,

I still envied her the view she had from her back deck.

I knocked a few times, but she didn't answer.

Was she there and ducking me, or could she be at the Boxcar? I knew that she was off tonight, but maybe she'd decided to stay and work. It might be tough being alone out here.

On a whim, I decided to check out the back deck to take in the view before I left. There was a full moon tonight, and I wanted to see the light dancing on the water.

As I climbed the steps so I could look at the lake, she said from the shadows, "Hello, Suzanne."

To my credit, I didn't pass out from fright, but I had to admit that I was a little shaky for a second. "I didn't mean to barge in on you like this, but we need to talk."

"Grab a chair and sit down," she said as she patted the deck chair near her. It was nicely lit back there with double shots of moonlight from the sky and also from the lake, and I had no trouble seeing her now that I knew she was there. Trish's ever-present ponytail was undone, and her blond locks cascaded around her face. She was wrapped in a blanket, and handed one to me as I sat with her. "It can get chilly out here at night, even in the summer."

I took it and draped it across my shoulders. "Thanks."

"It's beautiful, isn't it? James came back home with me last week for the first time, and he fell in love with it instantly."

"You two were dating, weren't you?" I asked.

I could see her nod slightly, and after a moment, she said, "It was brand-new, and we didn't want to tell anybody in case we jinxed it. He was having trouble getting Rebecca Link to accept the fact that they weren't together anymore, but he didn't want to rub it in her face by showing me off around town, so we kept it quiet."

"And you didn't have a problem with that?" I asked.

"Suzanne, you know how long I've wanted a good man in my life. Of course I wanted to tell you and everybody else in April Springs, but having him was more important than telling anyone about it. How did you guess? Did my crying at the diner this afternoon give me away?"

"I knew that you were upset, but I couldn't be positive it was because of the close relationship you had with James. I thought it might be because it happened so near to your diner, but then I found your personal telephone number in the back of James's journal."

"What were you doing with that?" she asked, a bit of ire jumping into her voice.

There was no way to sugarcoat this. "I've been trying to find his killer ever since I heard what happened to him. Grace is helping, too, and we're doing everything in our power to solve this quickly."

"I want to help you, too," she said as she started to get up out of her chair.

"Trish, sit back down. As much as I appreciate the offer, I'm not sure what you can do at the moment. If I need you, I'll be sure and ask."

She hesitated, and then asked softly, "Suzanne, if you're not here to ask for my help, why *are* you at my place long past your bedtime? You don't think *I* killed him, do you?"

"Of course not," I said. "But that doesn't mean that people won't be asking you questions, especially when they find out the two of you were dating."

"Are you going to tell anyone about it?" she asked nervously.

"They won't hear it from me, and you shouldn't even have to ask, but you know how people in April Springs can be. *Do* you have an alibi for this morning? Were you at the diner the entire time?"

"No, I slipped out the back door to see James," she admitted.

That wasn't good news, but we still might have an out. "What time was that?"

"A little before eleven," she said.

"When were you back behind the register?"

"It couldn't have been more than five minutes later."

"Are you absolutely certain about the time?" I asked.

"Of course I am. It couldn't have been later than one or two minutes after eleven that I was back, and the time stamps on the receipts will show that I was at the register by then. We each have a different code when we sign in so I know who to blame if something goes wrong." And then she got it. "I still can't believe that you're asking me for my alibi."

"It's not so much for me, but I want you to be sure when Chief Martin comes by here. It won't take him long to find your phone number in the back of that journal. James didn't exactly hide it. I'm guessing he'll be out here tonight, so I can't stay. He's already upset with me, but I promise that it's not going to stop me from digging into this. I can't believe how James and I

135

left things. I yelled at him about that stupid smoke from his fire pit getting into my donut shop, can you believe it? That's the memory I'll have to live with for the rest of my life."

"Actually, he thought it was kind of funny," Trish said softly.

"What? Did he say something to you about it?"

Again she nodded. "James said that he was going to build a bonfire next time just to egg you on. Suzanne, he cared about you. That little spat you had didn't bother him at all."

"Is that true, or are you just saying it to spare my feelings?"

I saw the whisper of her smile, oh so fleeting, in the moonlight. "Yeah, that sounds *exactly* like me."

"Okay, point taken. Listen, don't be upset when the chief shows up here. He wants to find out who killed James just as much as anyone else does, including you."

"I can't believe that," she said.

"Don't sell him short. I know that you cared for James, but the chief takes it personally whenever someone's murdered in April Springs. There are a great many people looking into this."

"Just not me," she said.

It was clear Trish didn't just want to help me; maybe she even needed it. "Okay, maybe you *can* help. Off the top of your head, who might have done it?"

"Besides Rebecca? You could talk to Murphy, and there's always his family in Pinerush."

"You knew about them?" I asked.

"James thought I had a right to know just how crazy he really was trying to get rid of a fortune," she said with the hint of another smile. "He told me the whole story out here two nights ago. It was really hard for me to believe that he was that rich, and I thought that he was kidding at first."

"Why did he come clean with you so quickly?"

"I asked him that, and he said that he wanted me to know that the money was never going to be an issue, that he was happier being a poor blacksmith than he'd ever been as an heir to the Pinerush fortune. I told him that I'd sign any document he asked me to, as long as we could keep seeing each other."

"I'm so sorry, Trish. I didn't have any idea that you two were that close. I'm surprised, to be honest with you."

"It just kind of snuck up on us, to tell the truth. We were just friends, and then one night it was raining and I got a flat tire. I was about to call AAA when James tapped on my window and offered to change my tire. By the time he was finished, he was soaking wet, so we went to his cabin so he could get some dry clothes. Suzanne, he was so gallant. We stayed up talking all night, and by morning the rain had stopped and something had started between us."

Trish had been looking for her knight in shining armor forever, and clearly James had suddenly fulfilled the role. It was an odd match at first glance, but the more I thought about it, the more I could see how they could be good together. They weren't exactly opposites, but I could see how there might be enough between them to make them mesh.

"It sounds wonderful," I said.

"It might have been. We just didn't have enough time to find out. I have the feeling that I could have fallen in love with him if we'd been given more time, but now I'll never know. Someone robbed me of that chance, and I'll do anything I can to help find the killer."

"Grace and I have come up with all of the suspects you've mentioned. Is there anyone else you might want to add?"

"Not offhand," she said.

As I got up from my seat, I said, "Trish, it's not good for you to stay out here by yourself when you're feeling this way. Why don't you grab a few things and come home with me? Momma and I would be happy to have you at the cottage."

"You don't even have to ask her first?" Trish asked.

"I'm sure that my mother would be delighted to have you. I have to warn you, though. I get up pretty early, but you can sleep in as long as you'd like."

Trish stood as well, and as she folded up the blankets we'd been using, she said, "I appreciate the offer, but I'll be fine here."

I took the blanket from her and said, "This isn't one of those offers that people make but don't really mean. We would love to have you stay for as long as you like."

That got me the second hug from Trish that day. "You're a good friend, Suzanne."

"So are you. How many times have you stood by me over the years? We both know that they are too many to count. Don't be one of those people who can give out favors but never take them from anyone else. It's okay to lean on someone else every now and then."

"I'll try, but it goes against my nature. Honestly, if I change my mind later, can I call you?"

"Sure, but try the house phone. I might be asleep, but Momma's a real night owl these days. I'll let her know that you might call."

"Like I said, I probably won't, but thank you again for the offer."

"Like I said, any time, day or night."

As I drove away from the lake house, I wondered if I should have been a little more insistent about her coming back home with me. Momma and I didn't have a lot of room, but there was always space for our friends in need. I was approaching the intersection to go back home when I spotted the police cruiser trying to turn into the lane that led to Trish's place. It hadn't taken Chief Martin as long as I'd guessed to track Trish down. Pulling the wheel of the Jeep over into a driveway just off the road, I killed my lights and waited for the police cruiser to pass me. Once he was around the corner and out of sight, I hit my lights, started my engine, and drove the rest of the way home. I wasn't sure how the police chief would react if he'd caught me at Trish's after what had transpired earlier, and I was in no mood to find out.

The rest of the drive home was uneventful, and I was happy when my headlights hit the cottage Momma and I shared.

Momma greeted me gladly when I walked in, as though the earlier exchange had never happened. That was just one of the things I loved about her. When it came to family, she never held a grudge or stewed over anything. The rest of the world might face her lingering wrath, but for me, she was always quick to just let things go.

"I heated up some of that turkey I made last week. I thought we'd make sandwiches."

"Excellent. Tryptophan is exactly what I need. Turkey always makes me sleepy. By any chance did you save any stuffing?"

Momma laughed. "I know how much you love it on your sandwiches. We've even got some cranberry sauce for a side dish."

"That sounds like a feast to me," I said. "Let me just wash up."

When I got to the table, I found a beautiful sandwich waiting for me. She'd mixed white and dark meat, adding just enough mayo to the homemade sourdough bread to give it some moisture. The stuffing had been piled on as well and was slipping out from under the bread. A tall glass of milk and a side plate with jellied cranberry sauce finished the meal, and I got my new phone out and took a picture.

"What are you doing that for?" Momma asked.

I punched a few buttons, and then said, "I just sent Jake a photograph to show him what he's missing. Sometimes I think it's your food that keeps him coming back around here."

"Don't sell yourself short," she said, but Momma was clearly pleased by the compliment. A second later my telephone chimed once.

I checked it before I did anything else, and all Jake wrote back was, "You're killing me. Take a bite for me."

I told Momma, and she smiled a moment before she said, "Suzanne, you know our rules. No phones at the table."

"Yes, ma'am," I said as I tucked it back into my pocket.

After we said the blessing I took a bite, letting the flavors explode in my mouth. My mother had learned as a new bride how to make a moist turkey, and she'd only gotten better over the years. The addition of the stuffing gave it all a blend of seasonings that was so much better than mere salt and pepper could bring to the meal. The milk was chilled to the right temperature, and the cool bite of the cranberry was the perfect complement to everything else. I shouldn't have eaten it all, but I couldn't help myself.

As I pushed my plate away, Momma said, "My, you built up quite an appetite after all."

"Sleuthing does that to me sometimes," I said.

"I do worry about you when you're investigating murder," Momma said.

"Hey, it's not like it happens every day. Most of the time I'm content just making donuts, hanging out with you and Grace — and if I'm lucky, Jake — and trying to get as much beauty sleep as I can."

"Not enough, in my opinion."

"Of which? Sleep, donuts, or time with those I love?" I asked as I gathered up the plates.

"I know you have enough with donuts, but the other two could always use a little more attention," she said.

We washed the few dishes together at the sink, chatting as we did. In many ways it took me back to my childhood; I had done the exact same thing beside her back then that I was doing right now. I hadn't realized how special those times had been when I'd been growing up, but I cherished the memories of them now. Leaving home and marrying Max — a professional actor I liked to call the Great Impersonator — had made me realize just how special my childhood had been. Though Momma and I were still trying to find the balance of living together as two grown women and not just mother and daughter, most of the time with her was good.

I kissed her good-night and headed upstairs.

Just as I was about to call Jake, my cell phone rang, and much to my joy, it was the man himself.

"That was just plain cruel," he said with a laugh when I said hello. "Was it as good as it looked?"

"Better," I said with a smile in my voice I knew that he could hear. "Think of it as another sacrifice you have to make for being so good at what you do. What did you have for dinner?"

"A cold hamburger and some flat soda," he admitted.

"That should be illegal. How's the case going?"

"From bad to worse," he admitted. "It's quite a bit muddier than I thought it was going to be. I'm afraid it's going to take some real work to solve this one."

My boyfriend, if you could use that ridiculous word for a grown man, was a topnotch investigator for the North Carolina State Police, and they never seemed to call him with the easy cases. "That's why you make the big bucks," I said.

"Oh, yes, I'll have you know that I'm a thousandaire. Stick with me, lady, and you'll go places."

"Having a lot of money doesn't always guarantee happiness," I said solemnly, thinking about James's life, and how he hadn't found any real peace until he'd turned his back on his wealth.

"Why do I get the feeling we're not talking about me anymore?"

I brought him up to speed on what I'd learned about James Settle's life so far. He scolded me a little when I came to the part about the journal, but we didn't have any secrets between us. Besides, I had a pretty good idea that Chief Martin would complain to him about me anyway, so I might as well spill the news myself.

"Wow, that *is* a lot of money," Jake said. "You'd never know talking to him that he was that well off. He was a good guy, wasn't he?"

"I thought so. I can't believe someone was cold-blooded enough to stab him in the chest like that."

"What I can't believe is that Martin told

you about it. You two must be getting to be real pals."

"Hardly. I think he told me just to appease Momma."

"Don't sell him short. He knows you've provided some real clues in the past, and he'd be a fool to try to keep you out of things completely. I wasn't all that crazy about you nosing around at first, but I eventually came around, remember?"

"I'd like to think there was more to it than just my investigation skills," I said.

"Stop fishing for compliments," he said with a laugh. "Listen, you need to be careful here. Whoever killed James clearly knew him, and I'm guessing that they knew him well."

"Why do you say that?"

"He let them stand close enough to him to stab him without him trying to defend himself. Besides, a metal skewer is like a knife. You have to be close enough to your victim to look into their eyes, and if you're not ramped up on anger or passion, it's nearly impossible to do."

"So, it couldn't have been someone who was paid to kill him?" I asked.

"It's still possible, but I'd have a hard time believing it. This thing screams that an amateur just got lucky and no one saw him kill James in a crowd."

"I still don't get that part," I admitted. "How could there not be any witnesses to a crime that was committed out in the open like that?"

"Right off the top of my head, I can think of at least half a dozen ways without really trying too hard."

"Like how?" I asked.

"Well, there could have been a distraction somewhere else in the park, or the killer could have made it look like he was patting James on the shoulder while the other hand was driving in the blade. Do you really want the entire list?"

I started to say yes, and then had to stifle a yawn. "No, I'd better not. It would probably give me nightmares. I'm so tired I might not get to sleep for at least four seconds after we hang up."

"Good night, then."

Now it was time for the most special part of my day. I waited half a beat, and then Jake said, "I love you."

"I love you, too," I said, and then turned off my phone and went to sleep. I couldn't always manage it, but when I could, it was the best way that I knew to put an end to my day.

QUICK CAKE DONUTS

When I named this recipe, it was less for the cake donuts I'm used to making and more about finding something I could make in my pantry on short notice. I was digging out the usual ingredients for some standard donut fare and happened upon a box of strawberry cake mix. These are tasty little treats, and you can experiment with different brands and flavors. This goes under the Very Easy file!

Ingredients

Mixed
- 1 1/2 cups (1/2 standard 10.25 oz. box) cake mix, your choice
- If you're baking, 1/2 cup additional flour, unbleached all-purpose
- If you're frying, 1 cup additional flour, unbleached all-purpose
- 2 eggs, lightly beaten
- 3/4 cup water

- Canola oil for frying (the amount depends on your pot or fryer)

Instructions

In a medium-sized bowl, beat the eggs lightly, and then add the cake mix, appropriate amount of flour, and water, mixing well until you have a smooth consistency.

Drop bits of dough using a small-sized cookie scoop (the size of your thumb, approximately). Fry in hot canola oil (360 to 370 degrees F) 1 1/2 to 2 minutes, turning halfway through.

Yield: 10–12 donut drops

Chapter 7

"I cannot believe it is so chilly out," Emma said the next morning when she walked into the donut shop rubbing her hands together. I'd let her sleep in, so she didn't have to get there until four a.m. It might not have sounded like much to some folks, but for us, an extra hour or two of sleep was like found money. "Suzanne, I thought it was supposed to finally warm up."

"It's coming soon enough," I said. "In a month we'll be *wishing* for a chill in the air."

"You might, but I love the warm weather. How are things going so far?"

"I'm just about ready to drop some donuts, so if you want to get the front ready, it shouldn't take me too long." I always made the cake donuts first, running through the entire process of mixing, dropping, frying, and finally icing them all before I did anything with the raised donuts. Those needed time to proof after they were initially mixed and kneaded by my floor mixer, and it always gave Emma and me some time to relax a little. We both liked to take our breaks together out in front of the donut shop no matter what the weather, but at that moment she had to leave the kitchen while I dropped the donuts. I'd instituted the rule when, once early on in learning the process, I'd let the heavy metal dropper full of batter slip out of my hands. It had dug a gouge into the wall less than ten inches from Emma's head, and after that, I wasn't about to risk it ever again. I refused to have it fixed so that it was always there as a reminder to me that I wasn't perfect, and that there was no such thing as being too careful.

After I finished dropping the last of the Cherry Bombs, my latest cherry-flavored donut, I called out to Emma, "All clear."

She came in smiling. "Wow, what did you put in those? They look amazing."

"I tried some Cheerwine in the batter this time, and some cherry Kool-Aid, too," I admitted. Cheerwine was a Southern soda, and the closest thing I could compare it to was a very cherry Coke, but it was so much more than that. I had a friend from high school who got ten cases every time she came home to visit from Maine, and I didn't blame her a bit. The Kool-Aid addition was a relatively new thing I'd been doing lately after seeing Kool-Aid-based donuts at our county fair. It really jazzed up the flavor and the color of the donuts, but I was still using it sparingly unless I was catering some kind of function at the elementary school. A donut that parents turned away from was often one that their kids adored.

As I iced the cherry donuts, Emma said, "I'll get started on the dishes."

She worked at the sink as I measured ingredients for our yeast donuts and turned the mixer on. After it had cycled through the mix, I pulled out the beater and covered the bowl with plastic wrap. Setting the timer for our break, I turned to Emma as she finished washing the last bowl. "We're just a well-oiled machine, aren't we?" she asked with a grin.

"It's great having you back," I said. She'd been gone, even though briefly, to explore the world outside of April Springs, and it hadn't taken long for her to decide to postpone living out of town until a little bit later in life. I'd take every second of her time that I could get, and if that made me selfish, then so be it.

"I wouldn't be any place else," she said. "Grab your coat. You're going to need it."

We walked through the gently lit front of

the donut shop and made our way outside. It was still chilly out, but not nearly so much as it had been when I'd first come to work. Perhaps our little cold spell was over and the end of spring could quit dragging its feet and finally warm things up. Once we were outside at one of the tables we kept there for patrons, Emma asked me, "Can you believe James Settle was murdered right over there?"

I involuntarily glanced over at the park where it had happened, and realized that if I'd only been paying attention, I might have seen it happen myself. How had the killer avoided detection from so many people? I'd seen that park, and it had been hopping. Then again, if it hadn't been very crowded, the act of murder would have stood out more. At least Terri and Sandy's kids hadn't seen the actual assault. That would have been a trauma they might never get over. "It's hard to grasp, isn't it?" I asked. "Does your dad have any theories?"

Emma's father, Ray Blake, owned and operated the *April Springs Sentinel,* our town newspaper. It was really more of a flyer full of ads than a real hard-hitting journalistic endeavor, but Ray believed that someday he would scoop the big city papers nearby and make headlines for himself. "He's following up on a few things, but you know my dad. He's got more ideas than Edison had patents, so it's hard to tell which theory he's going to settle on before this is all out. How about you?"

Emma had crossed the line with me a few times in the past regarding her father, telling him things I had wanted to keep private, so unfortunately I had to be a little careful with what I said around her when it came to my amateur murder investigations. "Who says I'm even looking into it?"

She laughed at that response. "Suzanne, don't tell me if you don't want to, but we both know you're investigating James's murder. How could you not? You two had a spat and the next thing you know, the man's dead."

"It was just a coincidence, Emma," I said simply.

"I know that," she replied, her eyes growing big. "Suzanne, I wasn't accusing you of anything. I never could believe that you'd actually kill someone."

"That's good to know," I answered, "but really, I don't have anything to share."

We were both silent for a minute, and then she broke it by saying, "If you're worried I'll tell Dad, you don't have to. After the last time, I told him that I'm no longer a source for him."

"Don't alienate him on my account," I said. It had taken the father and daughter a great deal of time and effort to get themselves on a good footing, and I hated being the cause for any rifts in her family.

"Don't worry; my mother has taken care of that. Funny, most folks think she's the quiet one and *Dad* is the one with the temper."

"Your mother has a temper?" I asked, not able to believe it. She worked with us on special occasions, and on the rare days I wasn't at the donut shop she filled in for me, with Emma in charge. It didn't happen often, but when it did, she was a real lifesaver.

"Not exactly. It's more like a very strong, silent energy that's nearly impossible to defy. I could never stand up to her as a kid, and my dad still can't. Anyway, she laid down the law with him. I'm only allowed to call information in to him if there's a fire or an accident, and he has to be my second call, no matter how much Dad might howl about it."

I had to laugh, knowing Ray. "He honestly didn't want you to call the first responders before you called him?"

"He says he was joking, but Mom and I

still have our doubts."

I was weighing the idea of talking to her about the case when I was saved by my timer. I trusted Emma when she told me her tattling days were over, but that didn't mean I had to tempt fate. Half of what Grace and I did depended at least a little on the element of surprise with the folks we talked to, and if they knew we were coming, I had the feeling that our questioning would be much less effective.

"Time to make the donuts," I said, alluding to an old television commercial that implied that it was a relentless task. They had that much right. It seemed like my entire life was spent making donuts, selling donuts, cleaning up after donuts, or getting ready to make donuts again. I was so happy that Jake was in my life, for a great many reasons, but one of the biggest reasons was because he made each day special and something to look forward to, even if we didn't get to chat or see each other.

"Sounds good to me," Emma said as we went back inside.

We made our deadline, which was a great deal easier to do since we'd changed our opening hours from five to six in the morning. I'd also made the executive decision to

156

close at eleven instead of noon, something that made my workday even more reasonable. It was still a pain getting up so early, but I doubted that many people cared about an afternoon donut, so closing before noon hadn't been a problem for me. As long as my customers clamored for my goods early in the morning, it was all the motivation I needed to get out of bed every day.

Our mayor, and my dear friend, walked in a little after six a.m. "Hello, George. How are you today?" I asked as I got him his standard cup of coffee.

"Well, I'm vertical instead of horizontal, so that's a good thing, right?"

"It is in my book. What kind of donut would you like today?"

He studied the cases of donuts on display, tray after tray of sweet goodness, and he stopped when he got to one in particular. I couldn't hide my grin, since I'd made it with him in mind. "You've got something called a Cherry Bomb? What's the secret ingredient?" he asked.

"There are two, actually: Cheerwine and cherry-Kool-Aid," I said with a grin.

"I'll take a dozen, but I have to get them to go," he said. "I've got a fool planning commission meeting this morning, not that I'm going to share any of these beauties with that ungrateful crew."

"Don't you want to taste one first? They might be a little strong. I'm still working on the recipe."

"You know me. I always say the stronger the better," he replied with a smile. "Besides, what Nan doesn't know won't hurt her."

"Has your secretary got you on another diet?" I asked, killing the grin I'd felt bubbling up. George was touchy about the weight he'd added since being elected our mayor, and I wasn't about to poke the bear. He and Nan were tiptoeing around the edges of a relationship, and I wished one of them would pull the trigger and ask the other one out.

"She says it's for my own good, but if that's true, why am I so miserable eating tree bark and rice puffed air?"

"George, Nan wants you to live a long time, and I have to say, I agree with the sentiment. Are you sure you want a dozen?"

"I thought you were in the business of *selling* donuts, woman."

"I am, but my friends mean more to me than even Donut Hearts itself."

He leaned forward and shushed me. "Don't let her hear that, or you'll be in for trouble."

I laughed this time. "George, do you really think my donut shop knows what I'm saying?"

"Don't tempt fate. That's all I'm saying."

"Pretty unusual advice from a former cop," I said.

"Some of the most superstitious people I ever knew were cops," he said.

Loudly, as though I were appeasing the spirit of my donut shop, I said, "I love Donut Hearts, and I wouldn't want to ever imagine my life without her."

We both stopped and listened, and at that moment, the refrigerator started chuckling softly. It was an old sound I'd gotten used to and most likely had more to do with compressors and seals than pleasure, but George grinned widely when it happened. "Don't say I didn't tell you."

"So, how many donuts would you *really* like?"

"I'd still like a dozen, but I'll take three. Nobody can fuss at me about that."

"You're kidding, right? Of course we can," I said as I bagged the donuts for him. Since he was being so good about it, I threw in a few donut holes as well, something I knew that he loved to snack on.

After I took his money and gave him his change, he lingered at the front for a second.

"Suzanne, I spoke with Phil about you digging into the blacksmith's murder."

"Phil?" I asked, surprised by the nickname. The police chief and the mayor hadn't ever been what you'd call friends to my knowledge, so I had to wonder exactly what had changed.

"We're working together quite a bit these days, and I'm getting to like him. When I was on the force, he wasn't my favorite person in April Springs, but he's matured over the years."

"Could his change of heart be due to the fact that you're *his* boss now?"

George shrugged. "I don't know, and I don't care. Anybody who makes my life easier is okay by me. Anyway, tread lightly there, okay?"

"George, you're not taking his side, are you?" I asked. We'd been through too much together in the past, and I hated the thought that I might be losing one of my staunchest allies.

"Of course not," he said quickly. "As a matter of fact, I'm most likely the reason he didn't rush out and arrest you when that journal showed up in his mailbox."

"He told you that?"

"We don't have any secrets around here," George said.

"And here I thought it was because of Momma," I said.

"Sure, that's part of it, but I had a word with him, too. Just don't make things any tougher on me than they need to be."

"You're not asking me to back off, are you?"

"Me?" He looked absolutely shocked by the idea. "I'm not crazy, Suzanne. I know you've made up your mind to do this, and I can't say that I blame you. All I'm saying is try not to rub his nose in the fact that you're snooping around yourself."

"That I can promise to try to do."

"Then we're good. Thanks again for the donuts. I'll see you tomorrow," he added as he shook the bag in his hand.

"I may not make any Cherry Bombs," I said. I had some old favorites that made the list every day, but there was always room for some experiments on my menu.

"I'll try to get by with these, then," he said, and then George was gone. As much as I appreciated the fact that he and Momma were looking out for me, there was a part of me that resented their actions, regardless of how altruistic their motives were. When we'd been married, Max had tried to do the same thing in his own odd way, and I'd grown to resent it from anyone.

Still, at least I knew that their hearts were in the right place.

It wouldn't pay to go against them if I could help it. After all, who would make the donuts if I were locked up for interfering with a police investigation?

Phil, indeed. I wasn't sure how I felt about that new development, but I was pretty certain nobody cared what my take on it was.

A crowd of construction workers came in just then, ending all thoughts of doing anything but serving them and collecting their money before they could leave. It would add nicely to my bottom line, and I wouldn't have to feel guilty about taking some time off later when my book club came by to meet in an hour. I'd thought about postponing it given James's murder, but we'd had to cancel our last meeting, and I didn't want them all to drift away from me. It had become a part of my life that I looked forward to, and I would have hated to see it end. Today's book was called *The Killer's Last Bite,* and when the group had first mentioned it, I had thought that it was a new culinary mystery, only to realize later that it was the latest title in a thriller series, *The Killer's Last . . .* So far the author had gone through *Kiss, Touch, Whisper,*

Sound, Sigh, and *Gasp,* and I had to wonder how many more books he had in him. I had enjoyed this one, and now I couldn't wait to go back and read the previous books. I loved when that happened; finding a nice inventory of books in a new-to-me series was pure gold.

Before the book club got to Donut Hearts, a man in a three-piece suit came into the shop. "May I help you?" I asked.

"I hope so," he said as he slid a hundred-dollar bill across the counter. "There's more where that came from if you're willing to tell me what you know."

I didn't make a move toward the bill. Had he waited until we were empty before approaching me? I had a feeling this man was up to no good. "What did you have in mind? I know quite a bit about a lot of different things, but there's one thing you should keep in mind; my recipes aren't for sale, at any price." That was a bald-faced lie, but I doubted he'd know it. For a hundred bucks, I wasn't sure what kind of information he was after, but I didn't think it had anything to do with my magical crullers.

"This isn't about your offerings here, as delightful as they must be. It concerns James Settle."

I took my index finger, touched it as

though it were smeared with mud, and slid the bill back to him. "Sorry, but that's not for sale, either."

He shrugged as he reached into his wallet and pulled out four more hundreds to go with the lone one still on the counter. "I have to warn you that if you're thinking about gouging me, that's as high as I've been authorized to go, unless you have something to say that is truly interesting to my employer."

"I wasn't dickering with you," I said. "James was my friend. I'm not about to betray his memory to you for money."

"You misunderstand," he said plaintively. "I'm searching for his killer. If you were indeed friends, you should be happy to help me. Why wouldn't you? You could profit from it as well as doing me a great service."

"Who are you working for?" I asked.

"Sorry, but I'm not at liberty to disclose that," he replied stuffily.

"Let me guess, then. It's either Anne Pinerush, or her son, Forrest." He flinched just a touch at Forrest's name, and I knew I wasn't going to help him. I could have used the five hundred, but not if it meant helping Forrest.

"I saw that. So, Forrest it is," I said.

"That doesn't really matter. Everything

that I just told you was true."

"So you say. Again, thanks, but no thanks."

He started to leave until I called out, "Hey, wait a second. Don't forget to take your money with you."

"You honestly aren't going to help me?" he asked.

"No, sir, I'm not," I said with a smile. "If you want a donut I'd be happy to sell you your fill, but I won't peddle any information about my friend."

He appeared to think it over, and then said, "I understand completely. I'll take a dozen of your finest donuts." As he said it, he pushed the money forward again. "Consider the balance your tip."

I shook my head. "Now you've done it."

"Done what?"

"You don't even get the donuts after that remark. Go on. It's best if you leave right now."

"And suppose I say no?" he asked as he collected the money.

"Well, there are a dozen men I could call to throw you out, but why should I deprive myself of the pleasure?" I asked with a grin. I reached down to retrieve the baseball bat I kept under the front counter to deter rowdies from acting up, and as I hefted it, I slapped the wood in my open palm.

"I'm going," he said, and quickly left.

I stowed the bat back under the counter as Emma walked out of the kitchen. "What was that all about?"

"How much did you hear?"

"Just that you threatened a customer," she replied with a smile. "If you were going to throw somebody out, why didn't you call me?"

"Do you think I would have needed any help?"

"Forget that, Suzanne. I just wanted to watch. What did he do?"

"He tried to pay me for information about James."

Emma whistled softly. "And you let him leave without even giving him a limp?"

"The first one's free," I said. "After that, I'm not making any promises."

"I wonder who sent him."

"I'm afraid I know. James's family is involved in this mess one way or the other. One thing's certain. I know that he wasn't here out of the goodness of his heart."

"Are you certain he's involved with James's family?"

I decided to bring Emma up to date, despite my worries about her sharing it all with her father. It would make my life much too complicated to keep anything from her.

After I told her, I asked, "Why else would he flinch when he heard Forrest's name?"

"Maybe he's had his own problems with the man in the past."

"Perhaps," I said. I knew that what Emma was saying could be right. If that were the case, who was this stranger, then? He'd made it a point not to offer me his card, and I got the impression that if I'd insisted, he would have refused. Could he be the mysterious cousin no one knew about? Somebody needed to look into that man's story, but I didn't have the resources to do it properly.

But I knew someone who did.

CHAPTER 8

I was happy when he picked up on the first ring. "Chief, a man in a three-piece suit just left the donut shop. He offered me five hundred dollars to talk about James Settle, but I refused. You might want to see what he's up to if you get a chance."

"Thanks, Suzanne, I'll get right on it," he said, and then hung up.

"Are you crazy?" my assistant asked me.

"What do you mean, Emma?"

"You just called our police chief for help. Are you feeling okay, Suzanne?"

"I'm fine. Think about it. I don't have the resources to track this man down, and even if I could, I can't force him to talk to me about what his interest is in James. On the other hand, it's Chief Martin's job to serve and protect us, right? I'm not afraid to give credit when it's due, and he's the most qualified person to find out what's going on."

"Wow, I need to write that down in my journal so I don't forget today."

I laughed at Emma and swatted at her gently with a towel I kept by the front register. "Don't you have dishes to do?"

"Always; it's a never-ending flow."

"Then maybe you should get to them," I said, smiling.

"Yes, ma'am."

I was still wondering about what the man's real motivations had been for asking about James when my book club came into the donut shop.

"Treats for all the girls are on me," Jennifer said as she walked in, waving a hundred-dollar bill around the room. She was a redhead, and the leader of our little group.

"Including me?" Sally Wingate said from the counter. "I haven't been called a girl in donkey years, but if you're buying, I'll take another bear claw."

"Why not?" Jennifer said. "We're celebrating."

"How about the guys?" Nick Williams said from one corner.

I was about to hush him when Jennifer put the bill down on the counter. What was this, my day for hundreds?

"When this runs out, cut us off," she said.

"Why the spurt of generosity?" I asked as

I put the bill in the register.

"I'm a brand-new grandmother," Jennifer explained happily. "But there's a catch."

"What's that?"

"You all have to look at little Erica's picture and tell me what a beautiful baby my daughter just had."

She pulled out the photograph and I saw they'd caught the little angel sleeping. "I'm sure that you won't have to pay anyone to say it. She's truly gorgeous," I said.

"Then be sure to save a donut or two for you and Emma," Jennifer said. "Hazel, surely you can break your new diet just this once."

Hazel was constantly trying to lose weight, always with very little success. She studied my display cases, and then said, "I'll have a plain cake donut, please."

"Are you sure that you wouldn't like one with chocolate on it?" I asked. I knew she was counting calories, but I also knew from past experience with her that Hazel loved *anything* with chocolate on it.

"Why not?" she asked with a grin. "You twisted my arm."

After my three other patrons were served their extra donuts, I saw Nick reaching for his cell phone. "You'd better not be calling your buddies and telling them about the free donuts," I said with a smile.

"Would I do that?" he asked, doing his best, and failing, to look innocent.

"I'm betting the answer to that is yes." I had visions of being mobbed, and after I rang up the donuts I'd given away, including ones for the other two members of our group — Hazel and Elizabeth — I rang up the total and brought Jennifer her change. "As much as we all appreciate the gesture, I don't want a mob scene here, at least not if you're interested in having our book club discussion today. Emma won't be able to handle the rush by herself."

"Would people really rush over here just for a free donut?"

I turned to Nick. "Do you have an answer to that question?"

"They would," he admitted with a smile. "Suzanne was right. I was about to call my buddies, and they would have called theirs, and who knows where it would have ended." He turned back to me and said, "Sorry about that. I wasn't thinking."

I smiled at him and got him another lemon-filled donut, his favorite, out of the case. "That one's on me."

"I won't say no," he said, laughing, and took the offering. "I'd better get out of here. I'm late for the gym as it is."

"You'll have to work out a lot harder today on our account."

"Happy to do it," he said.

I got Emma from the back, explained to her that the free donut run was over, and turned the front over to her. "Free donuts?" she asked.

"Jennifer was feeling generous, but we decided to limit the damage to her hundred dollars. She's got a new granddaughter."

Jennifer held the photo forward, and Emma said, "How sweet."

After we settled in on the best couch and chairs, Jennifer started off the discussion by saying, "*The Killer's Last Bite* is our book for today. I'll lead off by saying this entry was a little less spectacular than *Gasp* in my opinion, but still quite a bit better than *Sigh.*"

"I'll be honest with you," I admitted. "I didn't know this was a series when I started reading the book. I really enjoyed *Bite,* though. How does he keep writing about the same characters over and over again without getting stale?"

"I asked him that very same question last week," Elizabeth said. She loved e-mailing authors, and we were all surprised by how many actually responded. I was always interested in the stories she told of their replies, but personally, I thought the writers were crazy to answer her.

"What did he say?" I couldn't imagine what kind of mail they got, and I'd be afraid to open my in-box if I was one of them. I completely understood the ones who were recluses, free to write their stories without the prying eyes and probing questions of adoring readers. I was sure they appreciated each and every one of their fans, but how did they ever find time to write if they spent so much time answering all of their mail?

"He told me that the deeper he got into the series, the more aspects of his characters' personalities he could explore. He also said that bringing in new characters occasionally, even if it was just to kill them off a few books later, was a way to keep the writing fresh for him."

"That's fascinating," Hazel said as she took another small chipmunk bite of her donut.

"It is. But we were talking about *Bite.* Did anyone else find the culinary tie-in with this mystery a little distracting? I swear, there were more recipes than chapters in this book."

"I thought they were delightful," Elizabeth said. Whenever anyone said anything even remotely disparaging about one of our authors, she never failed to leap to defend them, as though they were all deep personal friends instead of the infrequent pen pals that they really were.

"What did you think about them, Suzanne?" Jennifer asked me. "You're our resident food expert, and I'd love to get your take on it."

"Hey, I'm a donutmaker, plain and simple."

"That's not an answer," Hazel said with a smile. She delighted in zinging us occasionally, and I hadn't felt like one of the crowd until she took a gentle shot at me one day.

"You're right, it's not," I said with a grin. "I liked them, but then again, I waited until I finished the book before I read them all. They might have distracted me otherwise, but as it was, going over them after I read the book itself was like finding that last cupcake in the back of the fridge that you forgot all about until you stumble over it at midnight looking for a snack."

"I adore cupcakes," Hazel said dreamily.

I saw Elizabeth hide a smile as she said, "I never thought of reading it that way. I'm a slave to the page for some reason. I feel as though I have to read every last word in order, but you know what? Next time I'm going to try it your way. It wouldn't take you out of the story that way, would it?"

"It seems to work for me," I said. "What about the character named Michelle? She's quite the siren, isn't she?"

"That girl put the 'bad' in 'bad girl,' " Jennifer said. "I just loved her."

"Me, too," I said. "I wish I had the nerve to say some of the things that come out of her mouth."

"Don't we all," Elizabeth said. "Sometimes I have a hard time believing that a man's actually writing these books."

"I've always believed that a good storyteller can take anyone's point of view and sell it to the reader if they're only willing to commit to it," Jennifer said.

I smiled softly as the women spoke, glad that this little group had found me. They'd stumbled into my donut shop looking for a place to meet in an emergency, and I'd been roped into their group by happy accident. Life was full of delightful surprises sometimes.

It wasn't until they were gone and I was still basking in the glow of their fellowship that it all dropped quickly away.

I was cleaning up one of the tables when I found someone had written a note on it with a ballpoint pen. All that it said was *KILLER,* but it was enough. I knew that some folks in town believed that I was capable of murder, but I hated having my nose rubbed in it like that in my own donut shop.

The door chimed, and I wondered if my accuser was coming back. It was Chief Martin, though.

"Hello, Chief," I said as I crumpled up the napkin. "Did you come by for one of my famous donuts?"

He self-consciously tugged at his belt as though grounding himself. "No, I'm not really all that hungry."

"So, I'm guessing this isn't a social call, is it?"

"Not so much. You asked about the man in the three-piece suit, and I wanted to let you know that I managed to catch up with him."

"Excellent," I said, surprised that he was willing to share the information, especially after what had happened earlier. "Who is he?"

"He goes by the name Thomas Oak," the police chief said. "Care to guess where he's from?"

"I'm willing to bet that he practices law in Pinerush."

"On the nose. As far as I've been able to determine, he's got only one client, and I'll save you the trouble of guessing this time. He's on the Pinerush family payroll."

"So, he's digging into this for the mother or the son. Do you happen to know which one it is, and why?"

The chief shrugged. "He wouldn't tell me. I found him over at the town hall, started to ask him a few questions, and then all he would do was hand me his business card. After he took off, I made a few telephone calls. He's on the up and up, at least as far as I was able to find out. Anyway, I just thought you might want to know."

"It's what I figured, but it's nice to get confirmation of it. Thanks, Chief. Are you sure you won't have a donut? One's not going to kill you."

"No, but if I have one, I'm going to want two. Two would lead to four to a dozen every morning, and I worked too hard to give it all up now. Thank you for the offer, anyway."

"You're welcome," I said.

Five minutes before we were set to close, a stranger walked in wearing blue jeans and a faded old T-shirt. He reminded me of someone, but I couldn't place him, although I knew that he'd never come into my donut shop before. I might forget a name, but I always remembered the face, and a donut preference. "What can I get you?"

"Coffee and a donut would be awfully nice," he said as he sat at the counter.

"You're in luck; we still have some of each. Any kind in particular you'd like?"

"I'm sure that whatever you pick will be good enough for me," he said with an easy smile. There was a rough handsomeness to him, and with his easygoing manner, I was sure that he didn't have any trouble with women.

"That's what I like in a man, low expectations."

He grinned again as he said, "Ma'am, I appreciate the interest, but I'm not looking for love at the moment."

I knew I blushed at his comment; I could feel my cheeks redden. "I'm not, either. I already *have* a boyfriend. He's a cop." Why did I feel the need to volunteer that particular piece of information?

"Well, then, I'd say that he's a lucky man. Does he work around here?"

"Actually, he's a state police inspector. He's out of town right now, but he'll be back any day."

"I'm sure he will." I grabbed him an iced apple cake donut, slid it into a bag, and then filled up a to-go cup of coffee for him.

After I quoted him the price, he handed over the money as he asked, "Did I say something to offend you?"

"What? No, of course not. Why do you ask?"

"I was just wondering why you were rushing me out of here so fast."

"I close at eleven," I explained. "It's the only way I can actually have a life."

"I don't blame you for that a bit, then," he said.

I started to give him his change, but he waved it away, so I put it in the tip jar. He wouldn't budge, though. After taking the lid off his coffee, he pointed across the park. "I heard that you had some excitement over that way yesterday."

"Actually, a friend of mine was murdered," I said.

The man shook his head for a few moments in silence, and then looked me in the eye. "I'm sorry to hear that. How close were you?"

"Close enough that I'll miss him," I said.

He took that in as well and then nodded. "Well, then, that's really all that matters, isn't it? What was the fellow's name?"

"James Settle," I said. After a second, I amended my statement to, "I guess James Pinerush would be more accurate."

"How well did you say you knew him?" he asked with one eyebrow arched. "You seem to be having a little trouble with his name."

"I knew him as well as he would let me. I never heard what his real last name was until yesterday after someone murdered him. All I know is that he was a fine blacksmith, and he took a lot of pride in his work. I was honored to call him my friend and own some of his work." I hesitated a moment, and then added, "I still can't believe some crazy killer took one of his own skewers and stabbed him in the heart with it. I've got an older set he made just for me, but to be honest with you, I'm not sure I'll ever be able to use them again."

"I know it might sound like an odd question, but would you mind if I saw them?"

What an odd request. "Why would you possibly care?"

"You make him sound like an upright kind of guy, and the world's sorely missing that kind of man. I don't know, maybe I'm crazy, but I just got a feeling that if I held one in my hands, I might get to know him better myself."

It was a crazy idea, and on my best day I would have refused him, but it seemed to me that the man had an honest and sincere desire to see some of James's work. What better way to honor the memory of my friend than to show it off? I called out, "Emma?"

She came to the door between the dining room and the kitchen. "What's up, Suzanne?" When she noticed the stranger, even though he was at least ten years older than she was, her hands went immediately to her hair, and the smile she threw his way was enough to brighten the room. That was my Emma, ever hopeful when it came to romance.

"Would you mind getting the skewers that James made for me out of the gadget drawer?"

"Be back in a flash," she said. If she thought the request was odd, she didn't show it.

Ten seconds later she came back out, holding the skewers in her hand. I took them from her, and then asked her, "How are the dishes coming?"

"I've almost got them done," she said.

"Well, then, don't let us keep you," I replied. For some reason, I didn't want her watching me as I handed the skewers over. It wasn't as though I wanted the man for myself. Jake and I had never been closer. Nor did I mind if Emma decided to ask him out herself. It was just something about James's memory that demanded some privacy.

Once she was back in the kitchen, I handed one skewer to him and kept the other for myself. He stroked the metal lightly with his fingertips, as though he were touching every mark and indentation James's hammer made on the metal. With a careful eye, he examined the skewer as though he were looking for a clue that held the secrets of the universe, and when he handed it back to me, it was clearly done with great reluctance.

"You're right. He was a fine craftsman," the man said.

I nodded as I held the metal tight. "If he hadn't made these just for me I would probably give you one, but I just can't part with either one of them."

He closed his eyes briefly as though he were blessing my decision. "You should keep them for yourself. They rightfully belong to you. Do you know if there's anyplace in town I might purchase some of his work? For some reason that I can't name, it moves me."

"I know he had some on consignment at the hardware store just down the road. I'd tell you to let them know that I sent you if I thought it would do you any good, but if Burt Gentry finds out I'm the one who pointed you in his direction, he'll most likely just double the price on you."

He laughed at my explanation. "I've known too many men in my life just like that. I'm Rome, by the way."

"Nice to meet you. My name is Venice," I replied with a smile.

"Now you're having a little fun at my expense," he said good-naturedly.

"Maybe just a little. I'm Suzanne. Yours is just an odd name, one that you don't hear every day, I mean."

"Granted, but it's still not as odd as my given name."

"Do you want to bet on that?"

"I would, but you'd lose. Brace yourself. Are you ready? It's Romance."

I chuckled a little until I saw that he wasn't kidding. "You're not serious. What kind of cruel joke were your parents playing when they named you?"

"Don't get me wrong. It's got a long and proud history in my family," he said. "My great-great-grandfather was named Romance, and I don't normally believe in co-incidences, but he was a blacksmith, too, just like your friend used to be. Maybe that's why I'm drawn to the metal. I've always had a soft spot in my heart for it."

"Maybe you're right," I said. "Are you passing through, or are you going to be staying a while?"

Rome laughed at that. "How do you know that I don't live around here?"

"Because I would have recognized you the second you walked through my door."

He smiled gently as he asked, "Do you know *everyone* in April Springs, Suzanne?"

"If I don't know them by name, I do by sight."

"Well, that's an impressive amount of knowledge indeed. Yes, I'm a stranger, and no, I'm not sure if I'll be lingering here or not. Could you recommend a nice place to stay if I decide to hang around a while? I don't want anything fancy like a hotel or an inn. What I'd really love is some kind of boardinghouse, if there is such a thing anymore."

"As a matter of fact, I heard that Mr. Quimby is renting rooms again. He just put the flyer up on the lamppost outside the day before yesterday."

"I'll look for it on my way out," he said.

Emma popped out in a rush just then, and she looked pleased that Rome was still there. "Everything's finished in back," she said.

"Excellent," I answered. "After you do the trays and sweep, you can go." I glanced at the racks and saw that we had just fewer than three dozen donuts left for the day. It was nearly impossible to make the numbers I sold match the ones I made, but I generally came pretty close. "Rome, if you'd like a few more donuts on the house, we can spare them."

"Thanks for the offer, but I'd better stick with one. It was nice meeting you both." He waved good-bye, glanced at Emma again and smiled, and then walked out.

"Who is that man, and how do you know him?" she grilled me.

"He's new in town, he may or may not stay, he's headed over to Mr. Quimby's about a room, and his name is Rome. Now you know everything about him that I do. If you hurry, you might be able to catch him."

"I'm on it," she replied, sliding the extra donuts into three boxes and then taking the trays in back to wash and put away until we needed them again tomorrow.

Rome was still standing there with his back to me when I glanced out again, staring wistfully at the park where James had been murdered. It was so sad, especially since Rome hadn't even known my friend. His empathy was strong, though, and ultimately it was probably the most attractive thing about him. I could understand Emma's interest in the man. Kind eyes and a ready laugh were two of the sexiest things in the world to me, and he had both in abundance.

When Grace walked right past Rome to get to the donut shop, she nearly brushed shoulders with him, and I found myself wishing that one of them would say something to the other. Grace had gone through a rather major shock not that long ago when it came to her love life, and I kept hoping that she'd find someone she could let into her heart again. Maybe it was Rome, but there was a good chance that it wouldn't be him. After all, he seemed to prefer blue jeans and T-shirts, while Grace loved getting dressed up at the smallest excuse.

Oh, well. A girl could dream, couldn't she? I knew in my heart that Grace would have to find her own way without any poking or prodding from me, but that didn't make it any easier for me to keep out of her love life.

CINNAMON DROPS

These poppers are a nice treat when it's cold outside, and they go great with hot chocolate. We make donuts year-round at my house, but we especially like them on those cold and rainy days we get too many of in our part of the South.

Ingredients

Mixed
- 1 egg, lightly beaten
- 1/2 cup whole milk (2% will do)
- 1/4 cup sugar, white granulated
- 1/8 cup oil (canola is my favorite)

Sifted
- 1 cup flour, unbleached all-purpose
- 2 teaspoons baking powder
- 1 1/2 teaspoons cinnamon
- 1 teaspoon nutmeg
- 1/4 teaspoon salt

- Canola oil for frying (the amount depends on your pot or fryer)

Instructions

In one bowl, beat the egg thoroughly, then add the milk, sugar, and canola oil. In a separate bowl, sift together the flour, baking powder, cinnamon, nutmeg, and salt. Add the dry ingredients to the wet, mixing well until you have a smooth consistency.

Drop bits of dough using a small-sized cookie scoop (the size of your thumb, approximately). Fry in hot canola oil (360 to 370 degrees F) 1 1/2 to 2 minutes, turning halfway through.

Yield: 12–16 donut holes

CHAPTER 9

"Did you happen to notice that man near the light post when you walked past him?" I asked Grace as she came into the donut shop.

"No, why?" she asked as she turned around and glanced outside. Of course Rome was gone now. "I don't see anyone out there."

"He was there a second ago," I said.

"Why should I have noticed him? Was he doing magic tricks or something?"

Emma had overheard that, and her enthusiasm was overwhelming. "No, but he has the dreamiest eyes I've ever seen. How could you miss him?"

"I must have had something else on my mind," Grace said, clearly amused by Emma's reaction to the man.

I noticed her straining her neck to look for him outside, and I realized that I'd probably gotten all of the work out of her that I was going to manage for the day.

"Go on, Emma," I said. "I'll finish sweeping up for you."

"Thanks," she said as she thrust the broom into my hands and bolted out the door.

"What was that about?" Grace asked after Emma was gone.

"Youthful enthusiasm, I'd say."

Grace smiled. "Ah, I remember it well. So, as soon as you're finished, let's talk about murder, shall we?"

"I'm all for it," I said. I put the broom aside and grabbed my marker board. After I'd erased today's specials, I asked, "I think we should put our list up on the board, don't you?"

"I know how much you like making them, so I wouldn't dream of depriving you of it," she said.

"Good. Then let's get started." I took the dry erase pen and wrote REBECCA LINK, MURPHY ARMSTRONG, MRS. PINERUSH, FORREST PINERUSH, AND MYSTERY COUSIN. "Is that it?"

"And we're not including Trish, right?" Grace asked.

"That is correct," I said firmly. "Her alibi works for me, so there's no reason to write her name on the board." There were four people in my life I knew couldn't be murderers, and Trish was one of them. The other three, in no particular order, were Grace, Momma, and Jake. Sure, there were other folks I doubted had the capacity for homicide, but I'd stake my life on those four, no matter how overwhelming the evidence might be.

"Good enough," she said, ending the discussion right there. As she studied the list of names, Grace asked, "Can you honestly see Mrs. Pinerush stabbing James in the chest with a metal skewer? I know that I can't."

"At first I thought that she might have paid someone else to do it, but Jake doesn't think it was a professional hit. He told me that too much was left to chance for a real killer to have done it. I suppose if her motivation was strong enough, though, Mrs. Pinerush could have done it."

"Suzanne, she told us that she practically raised James. Why would she kill him? From everything we've heard, he'd already given up on ever getting rid of that money."

"Maybe so, but we can't just cross her name off without a better reason than that."

"Okay, we'll keep her there." She tapped the next name on the list. "On the other hand, I have no problem believing that

Forrest could be a killer. There's something about that man I just don't like."

"He doesn't exactly come across as —"

"Human?" Grace suggested, interrupting me.

"I was going to say friendly, but that works, too."

"So, we're clearly not finished with either one of them, but I have a question. How are we going to get them to cooperate with us and answer any more questions? They can stonewall us all they want to, and they even have a butler to keep us away."

"Don't forget the fact that we have a spy working on the inside for us," I reminded her.

"Are we really going to ask Harry to do something that might get him fired?"

"Hey, he volunteered, remember?"

Grace bit her lower lip for a moment. "Maybe so, but I still don't like it."

"We all do what we have to do," I said. "Harry's a big boy, and I'm pretty sure that he can take care of himself."

"Okay, I get that. But before we go charging back there blindly, we need to talk to him again and see if he's found out anything new about what the Pinerushes have been up to. They must care about James, at least a little. Why else bring a lawyer into it? It means that they want to know what happened to him. At least that's one possibility," Grace said.

"What's another one?" I asked.

"What if one of them actually killed him, and they want to make sure that they covered their tracks properly? What better way to be sure that there are no loose ends than to do a little digging themselves, not to find the killer, but to be absolutely certain that the crime can't be traced back to them."

"You have a devious mind, my friend," I said with a broad smile.

"I just know how the rich can behave sometimes. Most of them don't think the rules the rest of us follow apply to them, and they do whatever they want."

"James wasn't like that," I reminded her.

"No, but then again, he didn't embrace the wealth, did he?" She looked at the list again. "Finding this mysterious cousin is beyond our limited resources, so we'll have to leave that to Chief Martin."

"If he even knows the man exists. I'm going to have to call him and tell him what we learned at Pinerush."

"I'll let you handle that," Grace said as she smiled.

"You're too kind."

"I hate this. It's so frustrating to have so

many suspects we can't talk to."

"I know, but there's nothing we can do about that. What we have to do is interview the ones we can, get the police to handle the ones we don't have access to, and hope that it all works out for the best. I admit that it's not the perfect situation, but it's the best that we can do with what we've got."

"Okay," Grace said. "That still leaves us with two suspects. Should we talk to Rebecca first, or tackle Murphy?"

"Let me make a quick call." I looked up the convenience store phone number, and after calling them, I found out that Rebecca would be starting her shift in an hour. After I hung up, I told Grace, "We've got time before Rebecca will be at work, so why don't we try to find Murphy?"

"Now it's my turn to make a call," Grace said as she took out her cell phone. "I tried calling him earlier, so his phone number is still in my phone's memory."

She held out her phone so I could hear Murphy's answers, and I got closer so I wouldn't miss anything.

He picked up on the fourth ring, and Grace said, "Murphy, this is Grace Gauge. How are you today?"

"Hey, Grace. It's nice to hear from you,

but I'm sorry; I can't talk right now. I've got hot iron in the fire."

Her voice turned the slightest bit girlish when she spoke again. "You're blacksmithing right now? Would you mind some company? I just love watching a man who works with his hands."

"I don't know," he said hesitantly. "It's kind of hot and dirty in the little smithy behind my place. I don't think you'd like it."

"Let me be the judge of that. Stay right there. I'll see you soon."

"Okay, that would be cool," he said, and then hung up.

"How do you know him, Grace?" I asked. My friend never ceased to surprise me, and when she'd started sounding like a teenager on the phone, it was all I could do not to laugh out loud and ruin everything.

"I used to date his big brother, remember? Every time I was over there to see Spencer, Murphy would hang around me like a puppy dog."

"Is there *any* man who can resist your charms?" I asked with a smile.

"More than can be named," she said. Looking down at her suit, she said, "This isn't going to do. I need to match your outfit. I'll be back here in five minutes after

I've changed, and then we can go."

"That's fine. I still have to run my reports and do a few other last-minute chores. Do you think Murphy would like a dozen donuts on the house?"

"I can't imagine him saying no. See you soon."

Thirty seconds after Grace left, there was a tap at my door. I was about to tell whoever it was that I was closed when I saw Max — my ex-husband — standing there with his tilted grin smiling at me.

"We're closed," I said as I smiled right back at him.

"Come on. Let me in," he pleaded. "I'm starving."

Against my better judgment, I opened the door. "You can have two donuts, but they have to be in a bag, and you have to eat them someplace else."

"What, no coffee?" he asked. The man was as handsome as ever, but to me he was like a brightly wrapped package without much of anything inside.

"I might be able to fill half a cup with what's left, but I'm warning you, it's going to be strong enough to arm-wrestle you."

"You know me. I love a good jolt of caffeine. I've been up all night, so that sounds like just what I need to get me going again."

"What's keeping you up at night, or should I even ask?"

"As a matter of fact, I'm working on something new and exciting," he said.

"Really? What's her name?" I asked as I bagged a few of his favorites and poured the last dregs of coffee into a paper cup. My ex-husband was a notorious womanizer before, during, and after our marriage, and it was a rare woman who could resist his charm when he cranked it up to full blast.

"I'm writing a screenplay," he said.

That was certainly news. My ex-husband was one of the least ambitious people I knew. "That sounds good. What's it about?"

"I'd love to tell you, but I'm afraid I'll kill the story if I talk about it. What do I owe you for all of this?" he asked as he held up the goodies I'd supplied.

"I'm feeling generous this morning. They're on the house. Good luck, Max."

"Thanks, Suzanne. I really appreciate that."

After he was gone, I ran the reports — which thankfully balanced just fine — and made out the deposit slip. A few quick swipes at the floor and a fast wash of the few remaining trays, and I was ready to start sleuthing. I was about to call Grace to see what was holding her up when she drove up in front of the shop.

I grabbed the deposit and a dozen boxed donuts, locked the front door, and then got into Grace's car. "What took you so long?"

"I've been ready for five minutes, but I drove around the block twice," she said.

"Why didn't you just come in?"

As she started driving, she said, "You had company, and I didn't want to interrupt you in case it was important."

I laughed at that as I directed her to stop off at the bank so I could make the deposit. "Are you talking about Max? Feel free to barge in when he's around any time you'd like."

"I don't know; you two looked kind of cozy. Is there anything going on there that I need to know about?"

I shook my head. "It's nothing like that. He's writing a screenplay, and I wanted to encourage him to work on something, no matter what it was. As for being chummy, the bad things that happened between us were a long time ago. I've been trying to get past it, and I think I finally have."

"I've heard that before," Grace reminded me.

"Hey, it's not my fault. I always mean it, but then he does something boneheaded and we're back to square one again."

When we got to Murphy's place — an ordinary ranch where he'd grown up — Grace parked in the driveway and we walked around back. The doors to the smithy were open, and we found Murphy at the forge pumping the bellows to get his coal fire burning brighter. Like James, he embraced the old ways of blacksmithing. I'd gotten a lecture from my friend several times on how modern blowers and air hammers had robbed the subculture of its history, but my eyes mostly just glazed over when he started talking about the golden age of blacksmithing.

Murphy stopped pumping the second he saw us, and I looked at his equipment. "You've got a beautiful setup here. Where did you get those handsome bellows?"

"I made them myself," he said. "James helped a little, too."

I remembered the donuts and offered them to him. "Care for a quick break? Sorry, but I didn't have any coffee left."

"That's okay. I never drink the stuff," he said, "but I wouldn't mind the donuts. Thanks for thinking of me."

As he took a raspberry-filled treat from the box, Grace asked, "Can we talk for a second?"

"I guess that all depends on what you

want to talk about."

"James Settle," she said.

His face clouded up a little. "There's not all that much to say. He was a good teacher. I liked learning from him, but I don't know a thing about his murder. I'm sorry. I liked him well enough, but I can't help you."

Grace said gently, "Murphy, we both saw the letter you wrote him, so there's no use pretending that you two were good friends."

The man's face, already ruddy, took on a new shade of red. "Where did you see that? Did he show it to you?" The last bit was aimed straight at me.

"Does it really matter how we found out? That was one angry note," I said.

He nodded. "I know, and you'd better believe that I regretted writing it the second I handed it over. James actually laughed when I gave it to him. He explained that he wouldn't have been so hard on me if he hadn't seen a lot of potential in me. We got past it, but it was still a mistake. I even asked for it back, but he said he wanted to keep it close to make sure he didn't forget how he'd acted toward me."

That was an interesting story. I just wondered how much of it, if any, was true. "Did anybody else know about it?"

"How should I know? I didn't tell anyone

what I'd done, but I can't speak for James. If he told anybody but you, I don't know about it."

"Murphy, where were you at the time of the murder?" Grace asked.

"Are you asking me for an alibi?" he asked, squeezing the forgotten donut in his hand until the raspberry filling oozed out like blood.

"It would help," I said.

"Why's that?" he asked as he studied us both in turn. "Are you two digging into what happened to James?"

"As a matter of fact, we are. Grace and I were his friends," I said. "Don't you want to know who murdered him?"

"Sure, but I'm not about to start meddling in something that doesn't concern me. All I know is that somebody stabbed him, but it wasn't me. I wasn't anywhere near the park when it happened."

"Can you prove that?" Grace asked.

"What happened to you, Grace? You used to be so nice," he said to her.

"I still am," she said.

He stood there in silence for a few moments, clearly getting angrier by the second. "You two need to go now," Murphy said as he tossed the ruined donut into the trash. "I've got to get back to work."

"Just tell us where you were, and we'll leave you alone," Grace said.

He reached toward the fire and pulled out an iron bar, the tip of it glowing bright yellow-orange. "Or you can just leave me alone anyway."

He didn't shove the hot bar toward us or make any threatening gesture with it, but the message he sent was clear just the same. Murphy was through talking with us, and there wasn't a thing either one of us could do about it.

There was nothing we could do but leave.

Walking back to Grace's car, we could hear the hammer strikes of metal on metal. There was an ominous pattern to the sounds, as though they were death knells from a muted bell.

"That went well, wouldn't you say?" Grace asked.

"Just lovely. He got pretty defensive when we asked him for his alibi."

"Imagine that," Grace said. "Just because he didn't give us one doesn't make him guilty, though."

"It doesn't scream that he's innocent, either, does it?"

"We'll have to try him again when he's not working iron," she said.

"It did make him a little aggressive, didn't it?"

She nodded. "Most men are still just boys inside. When they're doing manly things, they tend to act like children."

I didn't know if I agreed with that or not, but I wasn't about to debate the point with her. Grace had had her issues with men over the years, and while I'd been burned trusting Max with my heart, overall I'd had some pretty nice experiences with men. For some reason, though, Grace seemed to attract more than her fair share of trouble.

All we'd managed to do was antagonize Murphy.

I just hoped that we had better luck when we questioned Rebecca.

She was behind the counter at the convenience store when we walked in, and it was clear she had no idea who we were, or why we were there. Rebecca Link was short and slim, almost elfin in appearance. Her dark hair matched her eyes perfectly; they were a shade of brown so deep I thought they might be contact lenses.

Grace started toward her when I grabbed my friend's arm and said loudly, "I think the sodas are back this way."

She turned and looked at me oddly for a

second, and then winked. "You're right. What was I thinking?"

We went to the cases that had soft drinks, and as we pretended to study the multitude of choices, I said softly, "We have an advantage here we need to use since she doesn't know either one of us. Are you up for a little playacting?"

"You know it," she said with relish. In the past, Grace and I had pretended to be people we were not in order to get closer to our suspects, but we hadn't had the opportunity to do it much lately. "I want to be a princess," she said.

"Sorry, there aren't any princesses this time."

"Someday," she replied. "Okay then, who should we be? Don't tell me you want us to be reporters again. I'm so tired of that dodge; sometimes I feel as though I really do work at a newspaper."

"Well, that kills my one idea. If you can come up with something better that's also believable, I'll go along with you. Just remember, April Springs is a small town, and there's a good chance that we're going to run into this woman later. Well, we will if she wasn't the one who killed James."

"Okay, we'll be reporters. Where are we going to be from, *Iron and Forge*?"

"You know, that's not a bad idea. We can tell her we're freelancing a profile on James and see if she'll talk to us."

"Wow, the *truth* isn't as boring as our cover story, Suzanne."

"I know, but what are we going to do? We'll just have to make the best of it."

"Maybe, but I'm not sure how it's going to work on her. We could always just come right out and ask her about James, you know."

It was odd hearing Grace favor the direct approach, but I wasn't about to stop her. "Okay, that sounds even better. You start asking her questions and I'll follow your lead."

"This is going to be fun," she said with a grin as she grabbed a can of soda and made her way up front. What had I just gotten myself into? There was nothing to do now but follow her lead and see where it led us.

As she was paying for her soda, she looked at Rebecca and said, "Hang on a second; I know you."

"I'm here most nights. It's not like I'm all that hard to recognize." Her voice had a nasal tone that would drive me crazy if I had to listen to it for very long.

"That's not it," Grace insisted as she held a five-dollar bill just out of Rebecca's reach.

"You were dating James Settle about a month ago, weren't you? What a terrible thing that was."

She stared at Grace for a moment, and then said, "Where exactly did we meet?"

"My boyfriend and I ran into you at dinner once. Don't you remember?"

It was clear that she was struggling to, but it was obvious that she couldn't do it, probably because it had never happened.

Grace went on. "It was crowded and noisy, so I don't blame you for forgetting me."

Rebecca was openly scowling now. "I know that I didn't forget, because it never happened. James *never* took me anyplace fancy the entire time that we were together. Who are you, and what do you want?"

So much for Grace's fancy story. I decided to tell the truth, but with a twist. Standing behind Grace, I said, "You've got some nerve, lady."

"What do you mean?" she asked as she turned to look at me.

"If you wanted to ask this woman a question, why didn't you just come right out and ask her? I knew James Settle myself, and if you had, you would have realized he never would have gone anyplace like that."

"Sorry," she said as she grabbed her

change and left.

As Rebecca watched her, I reached down and picked up a random candy bar. "The nerve of some people," I said.

"I thought you two were together," Rebecca said.

"Why would you think that? Just because we walked into the store together?"

"It's not just that. I saw you talking to her in back."

I had to think of something to say, and unfortunately, what I came up with meant that I was about to throw Grace under the bus. "She wanted me to help her pick out a diet drink. Can you imagine asking that from a stranger?"

"The funny thing is that what she bought wasn't even diet."

I smiled at Rebecca as though we were sharing an inside joke, and then I said, "It is a real loss, isn't it?"

"How did you know him?" she asked me. It was pretty obvious she still wasn't one hundred percent certain that I was telling the truth.

"I work at a donut shop," I said, downplaying the fact that I owned it. I wanted her to feel at ease with me, and she might not if she thought I had money. All I had to do was show her my checkbook to prove that wasn't true, but this way was better.

She sniffed the air. "I thought I smelled donuts. For a second I almost believed that I was stroking out."

"Try getting the smell out of your hair before a date," I said. "Sorry about that. I wasn't thinking."

"What are you talking about?"

"I heard that you two just broke up," I said. "It wasn't that long ago, either, was it?"

"I don't know. It was long enough for him to find somebody else to replace me," she said as I stepped aside so she could ring up a few customers. "Can you believe it? He didn't waste any time finding someone else."

"I'm sure she was just a rebound," I said, knowing full well that Trish was nothing of the sort.

"She had to be. If we'd had a little more time to work things out, James and I would have gotten back together. I'm sure of it. He would have gotten tired of that waitress and come back where he belonged." Trish was no more a waitress than I was a cashier, but I let that one slide as well.

"Do they have any idea who killed him?" I asked once we were alone again.

"The cops? They're idiots. *I* could tell them, if they'd just ask me."

I leaned forward. "*Really?* Do you honestly know?"

She nodded. "It had to be that waitress. I'm guessing that he was dumping her, too, so she stabbed him so no one else can have him."

I said, "I heard that she had a pretty solid alibi."

"How could you have possibly heard that?" Rebecca asked me suspiciously.

I had to think quickly. "Cops and donuts. They go together, you know? I hear things. I don't mean to eavesdrop, but I can't help it."

Rebecca accepted that, so I followed up with a tough question of my own. "Do you happen to have one?"

"One what?"

"An alibi," I said.

Rebecca stared hard at me. "That's what the cops wanted to know, too."

"So, what did you tell them?"

Rebecca just shrugged. "There wasn't much to tell. I wasn't working, but I was nowhere near the park."

"But it's kind of tough proving where you weren't, isn't it?"

"I might be able to if I really have to."

"You can tell me," I said softly.

She looked around, and then when she

saw that the convenience store was empty, she explained, "I was getting my hair dyed at Cutnip. You can't see my roots, can you?"

"No, not a trace," I said. "Why won't you tell anyone that's what you were doing?"

"It wasn't all that I was up to yesterday, if you know what I mean."

What *did* she mean?

I was about to ask her when Officer Grant walked in. "Suzanne, I didn't know you shopped here."

"You know her?" Rebecca asked.

I made a warning face at the officer, hoping that he'd follow my lead. He shrugged and then said, "You can't keep a good cop away from his donuts."

"That's what she said," Rebecca said.

"Suzanne, if you've got a second, could I speak to you?"

"Right now?"

"I think that would be best," he said. "We can talk out by my patrol car."

I put the candy bar back and thanked Rebecca as I walked out of the store with the police officer.

We were two feet away from the building when he turned to me and asked, "What are you and Grace up to now?"

"Why are you asking me about Grace?

She's not with me, in case you hadn't noticed."

He grinned as he answered, "That's only because she's already circled the block three times. Unless you two are planning to rob the place, I'm guessing this has to do with James's ex-girlfriend in there."

I knew when I was caught red-handed. "Okay, it's true; you caught me."

He looked surprised by my admission. "You aren't even going to try to weasel your way out of this one?"

"No, not to you. Besides, we already told you what we were up to when I tried to give the journal back to you."

He held his palms forward. "I had nothing to do with any of that."

"Don't worry. We know that you didn't tell on us. The chief admitted that he found it all by himself."

He looked back at Rebecca, who was closely watching our exchanges. Officer Grant grinned as he asked, "Do you want me to put you in the back of the squad car to make it look good?"

"No, thanks," I said. "I think I'll pass."

"Then you'd better take off. The chief's on his way over here to interview her again, and it wouldn't do you any good for him to find you here."

"Thanks for the heads-up," I said as I waved Grace over to a parking spot out of Rebecca's line of sight.

Before I could go, he asked, "Just out of curiosity, did she tell you anything important?"

I shrugged. "She blames Trish, and after I told her that she had an alibi, I asked Rebecca if she had one herself."

"That was a little reckless," he said.

"Hey, these questions have to be asked."

"By the police, not you," he said, though there was just a hint of disapproval in his voice as he said it. "What did she say?"

"She said she was getting her hair done at Cutnip, but she implied that she was up to something else as well. If I'd had a little more time to push her, I might have gotten her to confess."

"Suzanne, I personally think you're crazy getting involved with these murder investigations, but I usually understand your reasoning. I know that you and Settle were friends, but that doesn't mean that you have to avenge his murder."

"Some folks think that I might have had something to do with it," I said. "My reputation is important to me."

"Your life should mean more. Just watch your step, okay?"

"Okay," I agreed. "Good luck in there."

"Thanks, but I don't need it. I'm not the one who's going to question her. The chief made it clear that he was taking the lead."

Officer Grant looked over my shoulder, and then he said, "There's the chief. You'd better hurry."

"Thanks for the warning. Come by and get a free donut sometime."

"I just might take you up on that," he said as I hurried over to Grace's car. I got inside just as Chief Martin drove up and parked in front of the shop. If he'd been trying to make a grand entrance, he'd succeeded magnificently.

Grace asked, "Should we hang around and see what happens?"

"I don't see why. He's not going to arrest her, and we can't afford to pop up on the chief's radar for a while. As discreetly as you can, why don't we leave?"

"I'd be delighted to. Just tell me where we're going."

"I will as soon as I come up with something," I said.

"Tell you what. Why don't I drive around a little until you're able to figure out what our next step should be?"

"Just don't keep driving around the convenience store," I said. "Officer Grant thought that we were robbing the place."

"We'd never do that," Grace said.

"Of course not. He should have had more faith in us."

"Everybody knows that there's no real money in a convenience store. If we were going to knock over a business, it would have to be a jeweler. Think of all of that gold in inventory and the cash in the safe, too. We'd make out like bandits."

"But we're not robbing anyone, right?"

"Who knows? The day is still young, and the night's yet to come."

CHAPTER 10

We'd driven down Springs Avenue twice when I finally decided on our next move. "What do you think about taking another trip to Pinerush?"

"It beats cruising the streets here in April Springs," Grace said. "Do you think we're still going to have access to the Pinerush estate?"

"Actually, I was hoping to talk to Harry again," I said.

"What makes you think he can get away?"

"Pull over and give me a second to call him. There's no use driving all that way if he's tied up at the manor."

She did as I asked, but after I dialed Harry's number, it went to voice mail after half a dozen rings. I decided to go ahead and leave a message. "Harry, call me when you get a chance. This is Suzanne Hart."

I hung up. "Well, that was a wash. Do you want to keep driving until I can come up with something else?"

"Why don't we drive out to the lake instead?" she suggested.

"Trish won't be there at this time of day."

"Probably not, but it would give us both something to do, and the worst-case scenario is that we get a pretty view while you're scheming."

"I'm not scheming; I'm planning our next course of action."

"Call it whatever you'd like," she said with the hint of a laugh.

After we got to the lake, we parked near Trish's place, and I asked Grace, "Are you up for a walk around the lake?"

"All the way around?" she asked incredulously. "Suzanne, that sounds suspiciously like exercise to me."

"I thought you worked out most days," I said.

"I already did this morning, and that included more miles than I care to think about on my treadmill before we got together. I'm not sure how much more I can handle today."

I scanned the lake and saw a bench near the water. "How about going that far? Think you could manage that?"

"It might be tough, but I'm willing to try if you are," she answered with a smile.

We were walking toward the bench when my cell rang.

It was Harry.

"Sorry I missed your call, but Mrs. Pinerush is in one of her moods today."

"Does she get that way often?" I asked.

"Since you two left, she's been biting my head off so consistently that it can be timed to every four minutes. I understand, though. She obviously thinks that it should have been me instead of James who died."

"What an awful thing to say," I said. "She can't really believe that."

"It's true, she does."

"How can you possibly know that?" I asked.

"She just said as much to me. She always thought that Jim and I were too close; we were the commoner and the prince. Only I didn't leave the manor; Jim did, not that anyone in their right mind would blame him. He got a bad shake in life, and my dad and I kind of took him in when things weren't going so hot at the house."

It was an odd way of putting it, the gardeners looking out for the heir apparent, if that's what James really was. For all Grace and I knew, Forrest could have been next in line to run things, or even the mysterious cousin. I had to believe that Mrs. Pinerush was in charge now, at least on paper. The way her son had pushed her, though, made me wonder if that was the case in actuality. "Who's running things out there?" I asked. "Is it Forrest, or Mrs. Pinerush?"

"That's a good question. Forrie's been trying to worm his way into power for years and Mrs. Pinerush hasn't been putting up all that much of a fight, but Jim's death has been some kind of catalyst for her. She may have let Forrest push her around yesterday when you were here, but she's not having any of it now. In fact, if you hadn't called me, I was going to try to track you both down myself."

"Why? What's going on?"

"Mrs. Pinerush would like to request your presence at dinner tonight. Actually, since she's gotten older, it's more like this afternoon. She would have normally had her butler call you, but she's got him off running another errand for her, so I had to do it myself. She must have found out that we'd already talked, though how she managed it is beyond me. Can you and Grace make it to the manor in an hour and a half?"

I considered the time that it would take us to drive home, shower, change, and still make it to Pinerush in time. There was no way we could do it, and I knew it. "How important is it that we dress up for the occasion? Is it better to be on time in jeans and T-shirts, or should we push dinner an hour later so we have time to make ourselves presentable?"

"Prompt is fine, early is better," he said. "As long as you're not fresh from the barn shoveling stalls, she can let just about any dress code violation go."

"Seriously? There's actually a dress code for dinner?"

"You don't want to know," Harry said. "I'll tell her you're coming."

"Great. Thank her for the invitation, would you? And if there's time after we eat, could we talk to you? We have a few more questions for you about James."

"I would be amazed if you didn't," he said with an easy laugh. "Like I told you before, if I can help, I will. All you have to do is ask. I'll be by your car when you leave."

"We'll see you soon then," I said and then broke the connection.

"I take it we've been invited to see the queen," Grace said.

"She's not even picky about what we're wearing, which is a very good thing. What do you say? Are you up for a dinner out?"

"I can face showing up like this if you can," she said.

I had to laugh, and Grace asked in response, "Did I just say something amusing?"

"You sell cosmetics. You are always a veritable fashion plate, while I'm rarely seen in anything other than what I have on right now. I have a feeling that you're going to have a lot harder time with this than I am."

"Point taken," she said, "but don't count me out yet." When we got to the car, she popped the trunk lid on her car and pulled a few things out.

As she put on a tweed blazer, I said, "Hey, that's not fair."

"I'm sure I've got something here that you can wear, too."

Grace and I shared many things, but clothing was not one of them. Our shapes were so different that about all we could both wear were scarves and gloves. "Thanks, but I'll take my chances looking like this."

"Suit yourself," she said. In less than a minute, she'd freshened up her makeup and at the same time she'd elevated it a notch or two to a more formal look than she'd been sporting before. "You really are good at that," I said as we got into the car.

"Practice makes perfect. Hey, don't sell yourself short. You've got talent, too."

"Like what?" I asked.

"I'm willing to bet that no one in April Springs can make a donut like you can."

"As far as superpowers go, that's not a very good one, is it?" I asked with a smile as she drove away.

"That depends on how hungry you are, and I just realized that in our haste to tackle our suspects, we forgot to eat lunch."

"We can't stop now," I said. "We're just going to have to toughen up and go without until later."

"We can't eat a full meal, but we have to get something to take the edge off."

I was about to protest when my stomach started rumbling. "Okay, but it can't be much."

"Trust me. I know just the place," she said.

By the time we got to Pinerush, we'd finished off the fruit-and-yogurt treats we'd picked up on the way. They weren't the small mass-produced fare some fast food chains offered, but a nice portion of yogurt and fruit that was fit for royalty. I was still a little hungry, but at least I wouldn't eat the bread basket when we sat down for supper.

"Come in," Stephen said as he answered the door. "Mrs. Pinerush is expecting you."

"Thanks," I said. He led us down a grand

hallway, the oak floors gleaming. The walls on either side were covered with portraits from generations long gone, and I felt as though I'd stepped into some kind of gothic novel. After passing several doors, we were led into a grand dining hall with a table large enough to feed twenty. There were just four place settings, though. I couldn't believe it when I actually saw my name on a place card.

"Mrs. Pinerush will be in momentarily," Stephen said, and then left us alone.

I held my name card up. "This is pretty fancy, isn't it?"

"Look at this china. It has to be a hundred years old."

"I wish you hadn't told me that. Now I'll be afraid to eat off it."

Grace laughed. "Then I won't say a word about how much those water goblets must be worth."

"I'd appreciate that." I looked around the room and couldn't help admiring a lovely large tapestry hanging nearby. "What do you make of this?"

She approached it, and then said, "It's just like one I saw at the Biltmore House the last time I was in Asheville." The Biltmore was the world's largest private residence, and a great many folks took tours of the home, especially around Christmas.

"You have a keen eye," Mrs. Pinerush said from the doorway. "This is the twin of one hanging there. Only two were made in this exact pattern, and we're fortunate enough to own this one."

"It's truly lovely," I said.

She seemed to shrug slightly. "In all honesty, it's been hanging there since I was a child, and I freely admit that sometimes I take its presence for granted. Would you two be seated?"

We took our places, and I glanced at the fourth name. It said "Forrest" in a fine cursive hand. "Will your son be joining us?"

"That was the original plan, but I've changed my mind. I'd like a little time to speak with the two of you first. We can chat while we eat." She reached beside her plate and picked up a small brass bell. After she rang it once, a woman in a maid's uniform came in with two plates full of what looked like duck, as well as a sautéed vegetable medley and wild rice. After the woman served us, she returned with Mrs. Pinerush's fare, a different meal altogether.

She must have noticed my glance at her plate. "I'm afraid that I can no longer eat the food you are having, but I hope that you enjoy it."

"I love duck," Grace said.

I just nodded. I couldn't say that I was all that fond of it, but I reminded myself that we weren't there to eat. Well, not *just* to eat. If this was what it took for Mrs. Pinerush to open up to us, I was willing to eat just about anything but snails. Rich folks could call them escargots all they wanted; I knew what they really were.

As I took my first bite, I was amazed by just how good it was. The duck I'd had before wasn't anywhere close to this in quality and I couldn't wait for my second bite.

"This is delicious, Mrs. Pinerush," I said.

"Please call me Anne."

I couldn't see that happening, but I nodded my acknowledgment anyway.

"First off, I must apologize for my behavior yesterday," she said.

I looked at her quizzically. "Funny, but I don't remember anything that you need to apologize for."

"That's gracious of you, but I was rude. Shock does that to me, especially as I get older. James really was like a son to me, and the fact that he felt free to rebel against my wishes endeared him that much more to me. I detest a sycophant, especially if we're related."

Was that last crack aimed at Forrest? It

had to be.

What Mrs. Pinerush, or Anne, had just said went against what I'd ever heard about her relationship with James, and out of respect for my old friend I couldn't see letting her claim otherwise. "Pardon me for saying so, but that's not the way I've heard it. You had James locked up in a mental institution. It doesn't sound to me as though you two were as close as you claim."

Her face darkened, and I wondered if we were about to be thrown out. Just in case, I stabbed another piece of that magnificent duck and gobbled it up.

Anne said curtly, "That was an unfortunate incident that we don't discuss here."

She might not, but I hadn't agreed to avoid the topic. "Sorry, but exactly whose feelings are you trying to save here? Call it what you will, but as far as I'm concerned, it was a monstrous thing to do," I said. I couldn't help myself; I just blurted it out.

Anne Pinerush was about to explode, I could see it in her eyes, but she finally managed to calm herself enough to speak. "I was under a physician's care at the time, and the decision was made without my knowledge or consent. The moment I heard what happened, I ordered him to be released immediately."

"Are you telling us that Forrest did it without your blessing?" Grace asked.

"I'm sad to say that it's true. I was livid, and James was so angry he never spoke to me again. I tried telling him that I'd had nothing to do with it, but from that moment on, he turned his back on his entire family. He was, for all intents and purposes, alone in the world after that."

"There you're wrong," I said. "There were a great many folks in April Springs who liked him, and a few of us even loved him."

She took that in, and then said, "If only I could believe it was true."

"She's not lying," Grace said.

Anne turned back to me and asked, "Were you perhaps one of those people who loved my nephew, Suzanne?"

"We were friends; just friends."

"There is no such thing as being 'just friends,' " she replied. "Every friend is a valuable jewel."

"I believe that as well," I said. "You don't have to worry about James's life after he left here. He was happy doing what he loved. The man was so passionate about blacksmithing that you couldn't help catching some of his fever for it."

"He was truly that good at it?" Anne asked tentatively.

"I have several of his pieces myself. He was outstanding," I confirmed.

"Thank you for that."

She was a little more receptive, so I asked, "Is that why you sent Thomas Oak to April Springs? To check up on James, and how he lived his life after he left here?"

She looked startled by the news. "What are you talking about? I'm afraid that you've lost me."

"Are you saying that you don't know the man?" Grace asked.

"Of course I know him. He works for the family's interests. But what was he doing in April Springs?"

"I sent him," Forrest said as he walked into the room. How long had he been lurking there listening to our conversation?

"Forrest, I told you that I wanted some privacy." There was a hint of steel in Anne's voice, and Forrest flinched a little.

"I know what you said, Mother, but I feel I need to be here to protect your interests."

"Are you sure you're not just looking out for your own?" I asked.

He started to snap out a reply, but then quickly checked himself. "I can assure you that I had the best intentions."

"Just like when you had James committed to the mental ward, right?"

"I was afraid for his personal safety. He was acting irrationally, and I didn't want him to hurt himself. I make no excuses for doing what I thought was best."

"Again, was it for his sake, or the family interests?" I asked.

"I won't stand here and let you insult me," Forrest said.

"Since you weren't invited," Anne said coolly, "it might be better if you'd do as I asked in the first place and leave us to our dinner and conversation."

"Yes, Mother," he said, and then started out of the room.

She let him get one step away from the door when she said, "One moment, Forrest. Is it true that you sent Oak to April Springs to dig into what happened to James?"

"It is," he said, clearly prepared for another tongue-lashing. "I felt it was our duty, and I take full responsibility for the action."

"I'm not scolding you. It was the right thing to do. Well done."

He nearly beamed from the praise. "Thank you."

"Now, leave us."

The smile dimmed, though it was not completely extinguished as he left us.

Once he was gone, she turned to me and said, "I will instruct Mr. Oak to pass on to you any information he discovers about what happened to James."

"He's going to tell the police, too, right?" I asked.

"Ultimately, but the first call he makes will be to you."

"Why tell us anything?" Grace asked, doing her best to look innocent.

Anne wasn't pleased by her question. "Come now, just because I'm old doesn't mean that I'm a fool of any sort. I have other sources in April Springs who have informed me that the two of you are quite the crime fighters."

"We may have been involved in a case or two in the past," I admitted.

"And now you're looking into James's death as well. Don't bother denying it."

"I wasn't about to," I said as I looked her straight in the eye. "I would do it for any of my friends."

"As much as I respect your altruistic motivation, may I add a little sweetener to the pot?"

"I'm not sure what you mean," I said.

"If you are able to solve James's murder, I will make sure that you are rewarded financially. I can assure you that it will be quite handsome."

"Thank you," I said, "but we respectfully

decline."

She was clearly not a woman who was used to being rebuffed. "May I ask why not?"

"You may. We do this because we feel compelled to. Our motivation stems from loyalty, not the desire for money."

"Why can't it be both?" she asked.

"Because it would taint what we're doing. We're strictly amateurs, Anne, and we make no guarantees. All we can do is promise to do our best to find your nephew's killer. We don't need anything else to push us on."

She paused. "I admit that I don't quite know what to make of that. Everyone in my circle is motivated by the acquisition of wealth."

"Hey, we don't turn over our regular salaries to charity," I said.

"But this is different," Grace added. "Suzanne is right. This is a matter of helping a friend who can no longer protect himself. It's the best way we know how to say a proper good-bye. Oh, some folks in town have been looking at Suzanne suspiciously because she and James had a rather public disagreement on the day he died, but that was the kind of friendship they had. He was a volatile guy at times, and Suzanne has been known to spout off on occasion herself."

"But you never do," I said with a grin.

"Maybe, but still not as often as you fly off the handle."

"Very well," Anne said. "I believe I'm beginning to understand. If there is anything I can do to help your investigation, either through Mr. Oak or my own devices, please don't hesitate to contact me."

We both agreed, and then Anne said, "Now please, finish your meals. I've ordered Chef to prepare a rather sumptuous dessert. I hope you've saved room."

I'd eaten nearly everything on my plate, but I nodded anyway. I'd find a way to sample some of the treat she had in store for us, and if I gained a pound or two in the process, I'd just cut back on my treats at home for the next few weeks.

I had an inkling that it would be worth it.

THE CHERRY BOMB BOMB

If you've been paying close attention throughout this series, you'll realize that I've been honest about the recipes that don't turn out anywhere as good as I'd hoped. I've been known to go through several versions of one until I get it just right for the books, but this one keeps eluding me. So, in honor of my tradition of including one bad recipe per book, I present my own version of the Cherry Bombs that Suzanne makes at Donut Hearts. Hey, I never claimed to be as good a donutmaker as she is! Make this one at your own risk! I wanted cherry extract instead of vanilla, but either my grocer doesn't carry it, or they don't even make it. The last time I made these I was out of cherry Kool-Aid as well, and I think that might give it just the kick it now lacks. Feel free to improve on this if you want to, but don't tell me about it. I'm retiring this recipe forever.

Ingredients

Mixed
- 2 eggs, lightly beaten
- 1/4 cup whole milk
- 1/4 cup Cheerwine (or other cherry-flavored soda)

- 1/2 stick (4 tablespoons) butter, creamed
- 2 tablespoons sugar, white granulated
- 1 teaspoon vanilla extract
- 8 maraschino cherries, diced
- 1 packet Cherry Kool-Aid (.13 oz.), optional

Sifted
- 1/2 cup flour, unbleached all-purpose
- 2 teaspoons baking powder
- Dash of salt

Instructions

In one bowl, cream the butter, then add milk, Cheerwine, eggs, sugar, vanilla, and diced cherries. In a separate bowl, sift together the flour, baking powder, and salt. Add the dry ingredients to the wet, mixing well until you have a smooth consistency.

Using a cookie scoop, drop walnut-sized portions of batter into small muffin tins or your donut maker, and bake at 365 degrees F for 9 to 11 minutes, or until golden brown.

Yield: 8–12 small donut holes

CHAPTER 11

Dessert was everything that had been promised, and as we were leaving the manor, Grace and I searched for Harry in vain. Why hadn't he met us outside as he'd promised? While it was reassuring to know that Anne Pinerush was on our side now, I still would have liked to speak to Harry to see if he could confirm what she'd told us at dinner. I had the feeling he'd know if Anne was telling us the truth, or if she was revising her personal history now that James was gone.

I spoke softly as I called his name. I would have liked to shout, but Stephen was still standing by the door, supposedly to make sure we made our way to the car safely. Why did I get the impression that he was spying on us? "Harry? Are you there?"

"Come on," Grace said. "We need to go."

I reached for the door handle of her car and felt something else there. What was it? When I looked closer, I saw that it was a folded piece of paper. I tucked it into my hand and got inside the car.

After Grace was off the grounds, I said, "Pull over a second."

When she did, I turned on the dome light and read the note.

I'm at the café. Come by after you leave the manor. Harry.

"What is that?" Grace asked me.

"Harry left us a note after all. How do you feel about driving over to the café?"

"Don't even mention food to me. I'm stuffed," she said.

"He didn't ask us out to eat. We're looking for more information, remember? I'm probably going to have sweet tea, anyway," I said.

"I could probably handle that," she said.

As we drove into town, I asked her, "Do you believe everything that Anne told us tonight?"

"She was an entirely different woman than the last time we saw her, wasn't she?"

"Maybe she's really telling us the truth," I said.

"It's possible, but I want to see if Harry's version agrees with hers before I make up my mind," Grace said.

"My thoughts exactly."

"I wonder what else Harry might have to

tell us?"

As we neared the café, I said, "I don't know, but I think we're about to find out."

After we parked, Grace and I started for the front door when I heard someone calling my name.

Harry stepped into the light. "I'm over here."

"Why are you lurking around in the dark like that?" I asked as we approached him. "Are you *trying* to give us both heart attacks?"

"Sorry, but one of Forrest's spies is inside eating. I can't afford to let him see me meeting with the two of you."

"Is it really all that bad?" I asked as Harry led us to a picnic table tucked away in the shadows, no doubt set up for folks who enjoyed eating outside during the daytime.

"I can't afford to lose my job, so why take any chances that I don't need to?" he asked. "Don't worry; we should be safe over here."

"What's up? I was surprised to get your note and not find you waiting outside for us," I said.

"I would have if I could, but things are escalating around the manor, and I have to watch my step. I had to see you, though. I just found out something that you need to know," he said. "There's a guy named

Benny who maintains the cars at the manor, and he drives Mrs. Pinerush into town occasionally. I've been hanging around the garage some lately to see if he knew anything."

"They actually have a full-time driver on staff?" I asked.

"Oh, yes. Anyway, Benny was changing the oil in Forrest's car today while I was over there getting gas for my riding mower, and he was staring hard at one of the logbooks. Mrs. Pinerush insists that she knows every mile put on those vehicles since the last chauffeur took her fleet out for joyrides whenever he had a chance. I asked Benny what was wrong when he kept staring at the records, and he told me that he'd just checked the totals from three days ago when he rotated the tires, and the mileages didn't add up to the entries."

"Explain why that puzzled him," Grace said.

"Well, Forrest put down that he went into Pinerush for a handful of business meetings, and Benny said there was no way he put that much mileage on his car just doing that. I had an idea, so I asked him for an exact mileage difference from what Forrest claimed and what he actually drove."

"How did you explain your curiosity to

Benny?" I asked. I didn't want Harry to take any chances on our account.

"I told him that I loved math puzzles, which is actually kind of the truth. Anyway, he gave me the numbers and I pretended to be ignorant about what they might mean. The second I left, I got out my road atlas and figured out that Forrest drove just enough extra miles to get to April Springs and back sometime in the last three days."

"So, he could have driven there and killed James without anyone knowing about it," I said.

"Maybe," Harry said, "but we shouldn't jump to conclusions. He could just as easily have driven to Rock Barn, or even Charlotte. We don't *know* that he visited your town."

"Maybe not, but he had a pretty compelling reason to come if he thought he was protecting the family fortune," I said.

Harry stood up from the bench. "Make what you will of it, but it was something I thought you should know."

He started to go when I called out, "Hold up. We have a question for you before you leave."

Harry turned. "What is it?"

"Was Anne really ill when James was committed to the mental ward? I mean bed-

ridden, not a cold or something less inca-
pacitating."

He thought about it, and then said, "As a
matter of fact, she *was* pretty sick around
that time. Why do you ask?"

"She claims that Forrest had James committed without her knowledge or approval.
What's your memory of the situation?"

He rubbed his chin for a full minute
before he spoke. "I can't exactly say why I
feel this way, but at the time, I got the
impression that she didn't oppose it.
Whether it was because she was sick or not,
I couldn't say."

That killed some of Anne's credibility for
me. I wasn't ready to accept what Harry
said at face value, though. "Think hard. Why
would you say that? Did you hear her say
something to that effect?"

Harry shrugged, and he was about to say
something when he stopped himself. "Now
that you mention it, I'm not really sure that
she was up and around at the time. I guess
she *could* have been sick. I'd have no way of
knowing if she was that bad off. The inside
help doesn't have that much to do with
those of us who work outside."

"Then how could you think that she might
have had something to do with it?"

Harry gave it a little thought, and then

said, "As best I can recall, I overheard Forrest telling someone that over the telephone. He knew that I was standing right there, because he made a point of shooing me away with his hands to make sure that I knew that I was supposed to leave. Forrest could have easily been lying about it, knowing that I'd never check with Mrs. Pinerush to see if it were true. Could he have just been covering his tracks in case someone asked me what I thought?"

"Forgive me for putting it this way, Harry, but I can't think of any delicate way to say it. Why would he be so concerned about what you thought?"

"Because I'm *just* the gardener, right?" Harry asked. The words could have been scathing, but his tone was light and airy, and I knew that he hadn't taken offense at the question.

"You have to admit that it doesn't sound as though Forrest would care about your opinion one way or the other," Grace admitted.

"Maybe not as one of his servants, but don't forget, Jim and I were always much more than that. If I thought for one second that Forrest had done it without his mother's blessing, I would have beaten the stupid right out of him then and there."

"You like Anne, don't you?" I asked.

He raised one eyebrow. "You've done that more than once tonight. Since when did you start calling Mrs. Pinerush by her given name? That must have been some meal the three of you just shared."

"She was like a different person during our meal," I explained. "I don't know what happened to the rather timid woman we saw the day before; she was gone today."

Harry nodded with a hint of satisfaction in his smile. "I was hoping she'd get her spunk back, but I hate that it took Jim's death to do it. Forrest tried to take advantage of her when she was in a bad way, but it sounds like she's getting a handle on things again. I, for one, am glad to hear it."

I looked at him and asked, "Harry, do you think that there's any chance Forrest could have killed James?"

To his credit, he didn't answer me right away. "If it meant protecting what he had? There's no doubt in my mind. He's got a cold streak running through him like a snake's back. Be careful around him. He's at his most dangerous when he's smiling at you. That means he's already planned how he's going to deal with you. It's just a matter of time at that point how and when you get it between the eyes."

"Forgive me for asking," Grace said, "but why hasn't he gotten rid of you yet? You must remind him of James every time he sees you."

"Our paths don't cross all that much in the course of a day," Harry said, "but he couldn't fire me even if he wanted to."

"Why not?"

"When my father died, Mrs. Pinerush promised me a job at the manor for as long as I wanted it, and Forrest isn't about to defy his mother that openly."

"And if something should happen to her?" I asked.

Harry shook his head. "Most likely I'd be gone before sundown," he admitted.

I nodded. "Thank you for risking it all just to help us," I said as we headed for our vehicles.

"No offense, but it's not for you. I'm doing this for Jim."

"You are a good man," I said.

"Maybe not as good as I should have been, but I did my best, and that has to count for something. Have a safe drive back home, ladies."

"Thanks. Don't forget to watch your own back."

Harry's grin was broad and open now. "Trust me, I do. It's *always* my top priority."

■ ■ ■ ■

As Grace and I drove back home, I asked, "There's a pretty compelling case that Forrest could have been involved in James's murder, isn't there?"

"What was his motive?" Grace asked.

"There had to be a ton of resentment when Forrest had to share his mother with his orphaned cousin, a kid he didn't like in the first place. We know that the two of them didn't get along for what turned out to be good reason. If we accept that as a possibility for a motive, then Forrest had the means, and from the sound of it, the opportunity. I'd say he goes to the head of our list."

"But we still have two other viable suspects," I said. "We can't forget about them."

"No worries there. Murphy and Rebecca are right up there as well."

"But not Trish," I said.

"No, not even if she confessed to us both and showed us the skewer she used."

"They already found that, didn't they?" I asked.

"I was just trying to make my point," Grace said. "Trish is off our list, but just because we don't believe that she killed him doesn't mean that Chief Martin necessarily agrees with us. I have a feeling that she's going to need more than a cash register receipt to get herself off the hook with him. She must be getting some real heat from him right about now."

"It might not be rock solid, but she does have an alibi. It's got to have some weight with the police chief."

"You would think so. I wonder if he's made any progress on the case that we don't know about?"

I looked at her and laughed. "You're not asking me to check in with him, are you? I think that might be over the line even for me."

"I wasn't suggesting anything," she said. "But you might hear things nonetheless."

"Momma and I don't talk about the chief or any ongoing cases if we can help it, if that's what you're asking. That's all on the Do Not Discuss list."

"Got it," she said.

As we drove, my cell phone rang.

"It's Jake," I told Grace. "Should I have him call me back?"

"No, go on and take it. I won't eavesdrop," she added with a grin.

I hit the Take Call button on my phone. "Howdy, stranger."

"Howdy yourself. How's your investigation going?"

"Isn't that what I'm supposed to be asking you?" I asked with a grin.

"Let's just say that I hope your case is going better than mine. Right now the bad guys are way ahead."

"But you'll catch them sooner or later," I said. "I have faith in you."

"I'm glad at least one of us does. Have you made much progress so far?"

I told him all that Grace and I had uncovered since we'd spoken last, and he whistled softly after I finished relaying what Harry had just told us. "What do you think, Jake? Should I tell Chief Martin about the mileage differential?" I asked.

"Suzanne, do you really want my opinion, or should I just tell you what I think you want to hear?"

"Okay, you're right. I know the answers to both of those questions," I said. "I'm just afraid if I tell Chief Martin about what I found out, he'll investigate, and it won't take much to track it back to Harry. It could be enough for him to lose his job, and I couldn't stand having that on my conscience."

"Hang on a second. Didn't you just tell me that Mrs. Pinerush offered to cooperate with your investigation?" Jake asked.

"She did."

"Then it's simple. Just ask her about it."

"What are you suggesting? Do you expect me to just come right out and ask for her help in proving that her son might be a killer?" I had a sudden thought. "Grace, turn around. We have to go back to the manor."

"Why, did you forget something?"

"I'll explain to Jake, and you can listen in, too," I said.

She did as I asked, and as we headed back to Pinerush, I told Jake, "I'm going to ask Anne for help, but not like that. What if I ask her for permission to interview the staff about James? I won't tell her what I'm really up to, but I don't think I'll have to. She was pretty supportive of what we are doing."

"That way you get the information yourself from Benny so that you don't have to implicate Harry. Smart move."

I always enjoyed being praised. Who didn't?

"Thanks."

"I'll leave you to it, then," Jake said. "I'll touch base with you tomorrow. Watch yourself, Suzanne."

"You, too," I said, and then hung up.

"That's pretty brilliant," Grace said. "How'd you come up with it?"

"I don't know. I must just be talented that way," I said with a smile.

As promised, Anne was willing to help. She gave us permission to speak with the staff still there and Grace and I headed straight for the garage. Benny confirmed what Harry had told us, and our friend was officially off the hook. I looked for him so that I could tell him just that, but he wasn't around as far as Grace and I could see.

Maybe he was back at the café romancing Lynette, but I doubted it. I would definitely have to have a word with him about the waitress before this was over.

Driving back to April Springs yet again, I dialed the police chief's number. When he answered, I asked, "Do you have a second?"

"Just about that. Is this about the murder?"

"It is." I told him what we'd discovered, stressing the fact that we'd dined with Mrs. Pinerush at her insistence, and that we'd discovered that Forrest might have had the opportunity to kill James himself.

"I'll talk to him first thing tomorrow," he said. "Is that it?"

"I was hoping you might be in a sharing mood yourself," I said. It was a long shot, but still worth a try.

He paused a few moments, and then said, "A single thrust to the chest killed James Settle. Whoever stabbed him either got very lucky, or they knew what they were doing."

"What does that mean?" I asked.

"I wish I knew. Anyway, there it is, for what it's worth."

After we hung up, I relayed the information to Grace.

"Wow, I can't believe he told you anything," she said.

"It wasn't much."

"Come on, don't kid yourself. He's sharing information with us. That's got to mean something."

"Just that we need to keep digging," I said.

"Any suggestions?" she asked.

"How do you feel about getting a trim?" I asked. "We need to go to Cutnip and see if Rebecca was telling us the truth about her hair appointment."

"Oh, no. Wilma Gentry's not touching a hair on my head. If you want the information, you're going to have to sit in that chair yourself."

"We could always just flip a coin for it," I suggested.

"The only way I'm willing to do that is if it's heads I win, tails you lose," she said.

"Fine, I'll take one for the cause," I said.

"Good, because that's the only way you're going to get me to set one foot inside that shop," Grace said as she headed toward town, and our next interview.

CHAPTER 12

It was late, so Wilma was off duty, but maybe that was for the best. I found one of her employees, Cynthia, finishing up with a client, so we decided to wait.

"If you'll both take seats, I'll be with you shortly."

We did as she asked, and I realized that it was a good thing to find her working the evening shift by herself tonight. She was the most conservative of Cutnip's stylists, and closest to my age. It also helped that Cynthia had aided a few of our investigations in the past, so maybe she wouldn't be opposed to doing it again.

After her client paid and left the salon, Cynthia looked at us. "Okay, ladies, who wants to go first?"

"We're not here for haircuts," I said.

"Shampoos?"

"No, not that, either. We were hoping that

you could give us a little information," I said.

Cynthia frowned before speaking. "Wilma doesn't like us talking about our customers. I assume that's what you want to know, right?"

"She doesn't have to know that we were even here," Grace said.

"Let me explain. We're trying to find James Settle's killer," I said. "Surely you want to help us find a killer."

"Of course I do," Cynthia replied. "I liked James. In fact, the last time I saw him, he had a present for me."

"Really?" I asked. "Do you mind telling us what it was?"

"I can do better than that. I can show you." She reached into her styled updo hair and pulled out a delicately crafted pin. "Isn't it beautiful?" she asked as she handed it to me.

I took it and studied the fine work James had done on it for her. The long and thin iron pin had been hammered to perfection and buffed until it gleamed like stainless steel. On one end of the pin was a small butterfly, also carefully crafted by hand. It was a far cry from the skewers he'd made for me. "James did this? It's magnificent."

She took it back from me and redid her

hair. I wasn't exactly sure how she did it — her hands had moved that quickly — but the new hairdo was completed in a heartbeat. "He was thinking about branching out into jewelry, and I was a tester for him. I came out beautifully in the deal, since he let me have the prototypes after he was finished with them."

"It's a far cry from rings made out of horseshoe nails," I said.

"Oh, he did those, too, but this was going to be his newest creation. I had orders ready for him from the moment I showed the pin around. Now he's gone, and I'm the only one who will have one." She started to clean her station as she added, "I can't force you two to leave if you want to stay, but I've got to clean up."

I was about to ask her again to help us, but before I could, she added, "If you want to chat about anything random that's on your minds, I wouldn't mind the company."

I nodded, finally getting it. "We heard that Rebecca Link was here at the exact time that James was stabbed in the park."

"She told you that?" Cynthia asked. "Why would she say something like that?"

I felt a chill go through me. "Do you mean it's not true?"

"She was here that day all right, but Rebecca left a good half hour before James was murdered."

"Are you positive about that?" Grace asked.

"I should be. I'm the one who did her hair."

"And you're sure that you couldn't have made a mistake?" I asked. "I'm not doubting your word for one second, but it's crucial that we know it's absolutely true."

She searched through a small box by her mirror, and after a moment, she handed me one of the cards. "For the past two weeks, Wilma has had us time-stamping these cards to prove how long each job takes us. It's been driving all of us crazy, but if it helps catch James's killer, I'm glad she did it."

I took the card from her and studied the stamp. Sure enough, Cynthia was telling the truth, and what's more, we could prove it. I had another thought. "Does Wilma still have that copier in back? I'd love to have a duplicate of this."

"She does, but I can't leave the front to run it for you," Cynthia said.

"I can do it," Grace said as she took the card from me. She winked at Cynthia as she said, "For the record, I never asked you for permission, and you tried to stop me, but I was determined to do it."

"Hopefully it won't come up," Cynthia said, and then bit her lower lip.

As Grace disappeared in back, I asked Cynthia, "Do you have any idea who might have killed James? Is Rebecca capable of committing murder?"

"I don't know. I can't imagine *anyone* doing something so terrible. It's true that Rebecca didn't want to accept the fact that James had moved on, but she seemed so sure that she was going to get him back. Would she have told me that and then gone out and killed the man she said she loved?"

"I see what you mean. Did she have any idea who James had moved on with?" I asked. I knew that Trish had been seeing him, but it was a question I needed to ask. For all I knew, Cynthia might have an entirely different answer to that question.

"Trish was seeing him, but then you knew that, didn't you?"

There was a hint of hurt in Cynthia's voice as she asked me that, and I felt bad for a few seconds. "I wasn't trying to trick you," I explained. "I just wanted to be sure we both came up with the same answer. Did Rebecca know about Trish?"

"If she did, she didn't say anything to me about it. It was almost as though the other woman in James's life didn't even count."

"She mattered to him. I'm sure of it."

"Trish didn't do it," Cynthia said firmly.

"You seem sure of that."

"Of course I am. Aren't you?"

"I am," I admitted, "but we've been friends for a long time."

"And I've been doing her hair for nearly as long," Cynthia said. "I know the woman, and she's no killer."

"Who else might have done it?" I asked.

Cynthia thought a moment, and then said, "Three weeks ago Murphy Armstrong brought me a few rings from James to try out. Murphy was upset about something, but when I asked him about it, he just grunted at me. I had the idea right then that the two of them were going through a tough time."

That just confirmed something else that Grace and I had learned, and though we had that letter to prove our theory, it didn't hurt to hear it from Cynthia as well.

"Is there anyone else? How about family?"

"As far as I know, James didn't have any family."

"Would you be surprised to learn that he did?" I asked.

"I'd be shocked," she said.

"They don't live around here, but he had an aunt and a cousin living in Pinerush."

Her eyebrows furrowed for a moment. "Are you telling me that James grew up there? That's hard to believe, isn't it?"

I almost told her that his family had founded the town, but I decided that the fewer folks in April Springs who knew that, the better.

Grace came out waving a sheet of paper in her hand. "That thing is a dinosaur. I had a devil of a time figuring out how to work it. Why doesn't Wilma upgrade to something made in the last twenty years instead of that relic?"

"She pinches pennies until they scream for mercy," Cynthia said.

"Anything else you'd like to add?" I asked as Grace returned the stamped original card to Cynthia.

She started to say something when the door opened and Betilda Enwright came in. The heavyset matron was clearly unhappy to find us there the moment she spotted Grace and me. "I had an appointment, Cynthia. These two will just have to wait until you're finished with me."

"We were just on our way out," I told Betilda with a smile. She wasn't one of my big fans, but she surely loved my donuts.

Betilda studied us both, and then nodded in approval. "Cynthia has outdone herself. You two look marvelous."

"Thanks so much," Grace said. "We owe it all to our stylist. Cynthia is just wonderful, isn't she?"

"She's very good," Betilda said grudgingly, as though the words of praise cost her per syllable.

"Thanks again," I said to Cynthia.

"Come again any time," she said, and then turned to her client. "What look are we going for this evening, Betilda?"

"I want to look just like Charlize Theron," she said.

I pushed Grace out the door quickly so Betilda wouldn't hear our laughter. The woman had as much chance of looking like the movie star as I had of sprouting wings and flying away. I couldn't see how Cynthia could do anything but fail epically based on the request, and I didn't envy her the task of even trying. Once again, I was glad to be a donutmaker, and not someone folks expected miracles from.

After Grace and I shared a few laughs at Betilda's expense, I asked her, "So, was Rebecca honestly mistaken about the time she was here, or did she lie to us on purpose?"

"I wish I knew."

"It's not too much of a leap to believe that the police chief is going to speak with Rebecca soon about her alibi, if he hasn't yet. I just hope that Cynthia doesn't let it slip that we asked first."

"She'll keep it quiet," Grace said.

"I think so, too. I just hope she does." As I stared off into the night, I asked, "So, where does that leave us?"

"I'd like to talk to Murphy again, how about you?"

"You just can't stay away, can you? Grace, the man has a serious crush on you. You need to be careful around him."

"Murphy's not a threat," Grace said. "I can handle him."

"I wonder if James thought the exact same thing," I said. I hadn't meant to be so blunt about it, but I wanted to be sure that Grace was careful around the man.

"Point taken," she said. "That's why I think we should talk to him together. The only problem is that I don't have a clue where he might be. I suppose we could try his little smithy again, but I'm not keen on going after him in his own lair."

"Me, either," I said. "He's got to do something else at night for fun. Do you have any idea where we might look for him?"

"No, but I know someone who might be

able to give us a hint or two."

"Who are you going to call?" I asked as she took out her cell phone.

She held up one finger and smiled. A moment later, I didn't have to ask. "Spencer, it's Grace Gauge. Yes, I know that it's been a long time. Two kids? Congratulations. Listen, the reason I'm calling is that I'm looking for Murphy. No, nothing like that. I just want to chat a little about blacksmithing. Of course I'm serious. Okay, thanks."

I grinned as she hung up. "You have some serious spunk, lady. I can't believe you called Spencer out of the blue like that. How'd you happen to have his number?"

"First I put all of our suspects in the memory on my phone," she admitted. "Then I added the folks who are connected to them in any way. I can't always do it, but when I can, it helps."

"When did you start doing that?" I asked, honestly curious.

"I just decided to do it while you were selling donuts this morning."

"It's an excellent idea," I said. "Two kids, huh? That could have been you."

"Maybe, but Spencer and I kind of played out our relationship in high school. You know me, once I'm finished with someone, there's no looking back."

"Doesn't that mean you're cutting out a great many of the eligible bachelors in April Springs?" I asked the question before I realized how it must have sounded to her. "I didn't mean it that way. I'm sorry," I added quickly.

"I know that," she said. "I'm not saying that you're wrong, but it does sound kind of brutal when you sum up my past dating experiences like that. Maybe it's time I lowered my standards and started going back through the leftovers."

I laughed at the way she'd put it. "Don't you dare, especially not on my account. Just keep being you, Grace. I know that you'll be fine."

"Said the girl with a steady boyfriend who happens to be a state cop and a hunk of a man."

I grinned like a lovesick schoolgirl. "He *is* handsome, isn't he?"

"Stop rubbing it in," Grace said. "Let's get in the car and go track Murphy down."

"Where did Spencer suggest we look?" I asked.

"I'm not sure that you'll believe me even after I tell you," she replied.

"Try me. I can swallow just about anything at the moment."

"According to Spencer, his little brother is

probably at the firing range in Union Square. Are you up for a little drive?"

"I'm game if you are," I said. "Who needs sleep?"

If James had been shot, Murphy's hobby might have meant something to the case, but he'd been stabbed. Still, it showed that Murphy wasn't all that afraid of violence if he shot off weapons for fun, and that was something, a new bit of information, to add to the mix of what we'd collected so far. None of it added up yet to allow us to definitively name the killer, but our investigations were often like that. We just kept adding new information to the facts we'd already collected, and sooner or later, we found our killer. I wished at times that it was a little easier than that, but if there was another way to detect, Grace and I hadn't stumbled upon it yet.

We found Murphy's truck parked in the lot at the firing range, just as Spencer had told Grace. The fact that Murphy Armstrong was a sport shooter made sense in my mind. After all, he worked with metal, bending iron to his will, or at least that's what he was learning to do. I knew that he loved to read by the books we'd seen in his shop, and if Spencer had said we should look in the library or a bookstore, I wouldn't have had any trouble believing it, either.

"How are we going to do this?" Grace asked as we both got out of her car. "We can't just walk up to him when he's shooting and start grilling him about James again."

"Not when he's armed, we can't," I said. "We could always just wait for him out here in the parking lot until he's finished."

She looked at the door to the gun range, and then back at me. "You know what? I like your idea better."

"Then it's settled," I said. "Should we go back and wait in your car?"

Grace pointed to one side near the front of the building. "I've got a better idea. Why don't we go over there? After all, it's a beautiful night. I think the chill's finally leaving us."

"It sounds good to me," I said.

We were there ten minutes when a car drove up. I didn't pay any attention to it, at least not until I saw who got out of the passenger side door.

It was Angelica DeAngelis, the beautiful owner of Napoli's, one of my favorite places to eat in the world. To my surprise, one of her daughters was with her as well. I stood and approached them, but Maria didn't notice me until I was right up next to them. She jumped a little as Angelica looked at me. "Suzanne Hart, what are you doing here?"

"I could ask you the same thing," I said. "Have you and your daughters taken up shooting for sport?"

"Not for sport. We have to protect ourselves. Two restaurants in town have been robbed at gunpoint, and my daughters and I will not go unprotected."

"I hadn't heard about that," I said. "Why just the two of you, then?" Angelica and her three daughters ran the Italian restaurant. I hated that she had to go armed to feel safe in a place that felt like a home away from home to me. "Where's the rest of your crew?"

"They're running the restaurant in our absence. Besides, we don't need them here with us, since either Maria or I am always on duty," she said. "We are sufficient."

"Speak for yourself," Maria said. She had her mother's dark and breathtaking looks, as did her sisters, and it was a wonder to me that no man had captured the attention of any of the girls yet. If the food hadn't been so delicious, I would have had to keep watch over Jake whenever we ate there, but he only had eyes for the ravioli. "My mother is pretty good, but I can barely hit the ground with mine."

"That's why we're here practicing," Angelica said. "Lots of women come. In fact, there's one from April Springs we see all of the time." She looked hard at me and then added, "Now, I've told you why we're here, Suzanne. How about the two of you? Are you getting in some target practice, too?"

"We're looking into the murder of a friend of ours," I admitted. I might have tried to deflect some of her scrutiny if it had been anyone else, but Angelica and I had a bond. I wasn't going to lie to her, or try to avoid her question.

"James Settle," she said decisively.

"Did you know him?" I asked, wondering how James had made such a broad impact in the short time he'd lived among us.

"No, but I understand that he was a good man. I hope you two catch the killer, but don't take any chances. It's a dangerous world out there."

"It can be," Grace said. "You two need to be careful as well."

"With our weapons or our restaurant?" Maria asked with a wry smile.

"Both," I said as I hugged them good-bye.

I was about to promise I'd come visit them soon, not an onerous promise to make at all, when I saw Murphy Armstrong coming out the door.

"See you later," I said quickly. Angelica got it immediately and she and her daughter headed off into the firing range.

By the time Murphy approached us, I was ready to start asking questions again.

I just hoped that he was in the mood to answer a few of them.

"What do you two want now?" Murphy asked the second he saw us. "Spencer told me you were trying to track me down. It's bad enough that you're harassing me at my forge, but now you're bothering my brother, too."

"We needed to find you so that we could apologize," I said. There had to be some way to diffuse the tension between us and still let us have a conversation about his late mentor.

At least he seemed willing to listen. "Go on."

"We weren't trying to attack you earlier, and if it came across that way, we're both very sorry," Grace said. She moved in a little closer toward the blacksmith, and Murphy didn't shy away. Grace took one of his hands in hers and continued. "Please forgive us. We just want to make sure that there's justice for James."

"I want the same thing," Murphy said. He didn't pull away, and after a moment, Grace did so herself. "Is there anything you might be able to tell us about who could have wanted to hurt James?"

"I've been thinking about that since it happened, and all I can come up with is something he told me last week."

That got my attention. "Why? What did he say?"

"He told me that if it weren't for women and somebody named Woody, his life would be pretty good."

What an odd thing to say. "That's not like him to dislike all women. Did he narrow it down any for you?"

Murphy nodded. "He said Rebecca was having a hard time letting him go, and James was getting a little frustrated about it since he wanted to go public with his relationship with Trish. Not only that, but he was having some problems with some woman named Anne, too."

What? Had Anne had contact with her nephew more recently than she'd told us? "What kind of trouble with Anne? Was it anything recent?"

"It didn't seem to be," Murphy answered. "I'm guessing that there was some kind of a long-standing feud between them, and every time he tried to resolve it, he couldn't manage to make it work. I got the impression that he regretted the rift between them and wanted to make things right; he just didn't know how to go about it, and it really bothered him."

"Who's Woody? Is that anybody you know? Maybe it was one of your customers?" Grace asked.

I tried to think if we'd come into contact with anyone named Woody during the course of our investigation, or even in daily life, but I couldn't come up with anyone. "Does that name ring any bells with you?" I asked Grace.

"No, I don't have a clue who he was talking about."

Vanilla Poppers

These poppers are also a nice treat when it's cold outside, and they offer a nice change of pace from the regular dense donuts we fry. The vanilla gives it an old-fashioned hint of flavor. The vanilla flavor might be subtle, so if you'd like an extra pop, double the amount to 3 teaspoons.

Ingredients

Mixed
- 3 eggs, lightly beaten
- 1 cup sugar, white granulated
- 1 cup buttermilk
- 1/2 cup sour cream
- 1/8 cup oil (canola is my favorite)
- 1 1/2 teaspoons vanilla extract

Sifted
- 3 to 3 1/2 cups flour, unbleached all-purpose
- 1 teaspoon baking powder
- Dash of salt

- Canola oil for frying (the amount depends on your pot or fryer)

Instructions

In one bowl, beat the eggs lightly, and then add the sugar, buttermilk, sour cream, oil, and vanilla. In a separate bowl, sift together the flour, baking powder, and salt.

Add the dry ingredients to the wet, mixing well until you have a smooth consistency.

Drop bits of dough using a small-sized cookie scoop (the size of your thumb, approximately). Fry in hot canola oil (360 to 370 degrees F) 1 1/2 to 2 minutes, turning halfway through.

Yield: 10–12 donut drops

CHAPTER 13

And then I remembered James's skewed sense of humor. It would be just like him to give his cousin Forrest a nickname like Woody. "I know who he was talking about," I said.

"Who?"

"Forrest."

She shook her head. "You have to be right. I should have gotten that, too."

"Who is this Forrest guy?" Murphy asked.

"He's someone who was connected once to James's life," I said, not wanting to go into too much detail. "Can you remember anything he said about Woody in particular?"

"Just that he wasn't going to get what he wanted if James had anything to say about it."

That could have meant a dozen different things, but I had the feeling every one of them led straight back to the family fortune.

"How long ago did he say it?"

"Two weeks ago, maybe even ten days, but I know that it wasn't much past that."

"So, they were in touch recently."

"I guess so. The day they spoke on the phone, I was working on some hinges with James, and he took the hammer from me and wailed on that iron like it owed him money. He felt better after he got out some of his aggression, but I wouldn't have wanted to be Woody or Forrest or whatever that guy's name was."

"Is there anything else you can tell us that might help?" Grace asked in that soft and pliant voice I'd heard her use to get information in the past.

"Sorry, but that's it. So, you two don't think I killed him anymore, is that right?"

"We'd still love to hear your alibi just so we can cross your name off our list once and for all," Grace said gently. "I want to believe you, Murphy; I really do. Help me do that, won't you?"

He looked down at his feet, and then he finally said, "The truth is, I'm afraid you're going to think less of me when I tell you."

"We won't judge you, no matter what you were doing," I said. What kind of dark secret was this man hiding? Could it really be better being considered a murder suspect than admitting where he'd been when James had been murdered? I suddenly wasn't so sure that I wanted to hear what he had to say, and I hoped that I didn't live to regret my promise.

"Okay, but it goes no farther than this," Murphy said. "Truth be told, I was taking a class when James was stabbed."

"A class?" I asked. "What's wrong with that?"

"It was tap, okay?"

I kept repeating, *I will not smile, I will not smile,* over and over again, and somehow I managed to keep it buried down deep inside me.

"I didn't know you wanted to be a dancer," Grace said.

"It was an introductory thing, and I thought I'd give it a shot. I saw Fred Astaire in an old movie a few weeks ago and I thought he looked cool. I'll tell you one thing; it's a lot tougher than it looks."

"Why don't you want anyone to know?" I asked. "I can understand you being a little shy about it in general, but after all, this is a murder investigation."

"Yours is an unofficial one, though," he said. "How's it going to look to all of April Springs if a blacksmith was taking classes so he could be lighter on his feet?"

"I think it says a lot about you," Grace said, "and it's all good."

"Seriously? You're not just yanking my chain, are you?"

"I'm being perfectly honest with you," she said. "I know that it's not ballroom dancing, but I love a man who can dance."

"Anyway, now you know why I didn't want to tell anybody."

"Hang on a second," I said. "Are you telling me that you refused to tell the police where you were because you were afraid they might make fun of you? Do you understand how crazy that sounds on the face of it?"

"Hey, my reputation around here is about all I have these days."

"It's safe with us," I reassured him, "but you've *got* to tell Chief Martin."

"You mean right now?" he asked.

"It's as good a time as any. The sooner you can prove where you were, the quicker your name will go off his list."

"I don't know," Murphy said. "I'm not sure that I can bring myself to do it."

I was about to scold him when Grace asked, "Would you like me to go with you?"

"Would you?" he asked as he looked at her with hope in his gaze.

"Why not? On the way over, you can tell

me all about that class. It sounds like fun." She turned to me and asked, "Would you like to come, too, Suzanne?"

"I don't have much choice, do I? You drove us here, remember?"

She retrieved her keys from her purse and handed them to me. "Don't worry about it. You can take my car. I'll catch a ride with Murphy and pick it up at your place later."

"That's a company car, Grace. Don't you think they might get a little miffed if something happened to it while I was driving instead of you?"

"First of all, nothing's going to happen, and even if it does, you're on my insurance plan for it."

"How did that happen?" It was certainly news to me.

"Everyone else was putting their spouses' names down, and I didn't want to leave it blank, so I covered you, too."

"That's the sweetest *and* the oddest thing I've heard in years," I said.

"Let's not get choked up about it," she said. "I'll see you later."

"Good-bye," I said, and Grace left with Murphy to head back to town so they could go to the police department. I started having second thoughts in a big way the second they pulled out of the parking lot. What if

Murphy was lying to us? What if he wasn't taking dance lessons, tap or otherwise? Had it been a ploy to trap Grace, or was he just going to take advantage of the situation? I grabbed my phone as I got into Grace's car.

I could see Murphy's taillights in the dark, but they were fading fast.

"I'm right behind you," I said as I took off, flashing my lights as I sped to keep up with them.

"Suzanne, you don't have to do that."

"I know I don't, but I want to. Tell Murphy to ease up on the gas, would you? He's not trying to lose me, is he?"

I heard her ask him to slow down, and for a heart-stopping moment, I thought he was speeding up, but he backed off the gas and soon I was just behind them.

"Tell her you're safe with me," I heard Murphy say to Grace.

At the moment, I wasn't in any mood to believe him. "It's not that. I just want to be sure nothing happens to your car," I told Grace.

"She's worried about my company car," Grace told him, and in the headlights I could see Murphy nodding his head.

"She probably should be. I'm guessing the deductible on that car is more than her entire Jeep is worth. She'd *better* be careful."

I'd used it as an excuse, but now I found myself worrying about the vehicle. Why did he have to put that thought in my head? Was it payback for me following them?

"I am," I said.

"Suzanne, my cell phone battery is getting low, so I'm signing off. We'll see you back in town."

I couldn't exactly make her stay on the line, but I wasn't about to let them get away, either. Murphy suddenly sped up, and I felt my heart leap into my throat, but he tapped the brakes as he eased off the gas and I realized that he was just having a bit of fun with me.

Some fun.

By the time we got back into town and parked in front of the police station, I was a nervous wreck. When I got out, I saw that Grace and Murphy were laughing about something. All I had to say was that it had better not be me.

"Here are your keys," I said as I handed them to Grace.

"Don't you want to drive it home?"

"Thanks anyway, but it's a nice night. I think I'll walk."

I started to go when Grace called out,

"Suzanne, hang on a second."

I waited for her, and as she approached, she said, "Listen, I told him that it wasn't funny, but he was kind of giddy having me in the car with him. I think he was trying to impress me."

"And did he?" I asked. "Grace, he's not exactly your type, and that's not even taking into account the fact that he's still a murder suspect until Chief Martin clears him. Maybe you'd better wait a while until you get too involved with him."

"We're not going out or anything," Grace said. "I just thought that it was important that he talk to Chief Martin, so I did the only thing I could to make sure of it. That's all there is to it."

"Hey, it's fine with me either way. Just wait until he's cleared first."

"You've always looked out for me, Suzanne," she said.

"Hey, that's what friends are for." I looked over her shoulder and saw Officer Grant talking to Murphy.

"Now I feel better," I said.

"What, because we're going to have a police escort into the building?" Grace asked with a smile.

"That's exactly right. I don't care how silly it sounds. I'm still having a hard time believing that Murphy is innocent."

"The chief will clear it up soon enough. Now go on. I can handle this."

"Okay," I said. "Call me when you get home, though, okay?"

"Yes, Mother," she said with a laugh.

"You could do worse," I said as I waved to Officer Grant and took off on foot back to the cottage. I decided at the last second to cut through the park, and as I did, I couldn't help but glance at the spot where James had been murdered. It really had taken the nerves of a cat burglar to kill him out there in the open. How had the murderer managed it? What act had allowed them to approach James and get close enough to stab him in the heart? I was still wondering about it when I walked past the Patriot's Tree and up the steps to the cottage that Momma and I shared.

"Wow, that smells wonderful," I said as I walked in the front door. Even though I'd recently eaten at Anne Pinerush's place, I found that I was a little hungry again. It looked as though this was going to be one of those banner days when I managed to get four meals instead of the standard three.

Momma turned and looked pleased to see me as I walked into the kitchen. "Suzanne, your timing is perfect." She looked past me as she asked, "Is Grace with you?"

"No, she's at the police station," I said, without realizing how it must have sounded to my mother.

"How on earth did she manage to get arrested and you got away scot-free?"

I had to laugh. "Thanks for the vote of confidence, Momma. My guilt was never in question, was it?"

"Let's face it, Suzanne; you're usually the instigator. Is that why you came home? If you need bail money, I've got a stash here just for that reason."

As often as she'd told the joke, I still had to wonder if it might be true. My mother was a spirited woman, and I liked to think that I got some of that from her.

"No, she went in with Murphy Armstrong to give him some moral support."

"*Murphy* killed James?" my mother asked, clearly shocked by the idea.

"No, as a matter of fact, it looks as though he's in the clear. He didn't want to give Chief Martin his alibi, though, so Grace decided to go along just to make sure that he did. Murphy's had a crush on her since she dated his older brother back in high school, and I swear that man would do just about anything he thought might please her."

"Why did he not want to give Phillip his alibi?" Momma asked.

I wasn't sure what kind of confidentiality Murphy had a right to expect from Chief Martin, but I had a feeling that Momma would know soon enough. "I'll tell you, but you can't tell anyone else. Agreed?"

"That's fine with me," she answered quickly.

"He was taking tap lessons," I said with a smile.

"That big man dancing around nimbly in tap shoes?" Momma asked.

"That's what he claims."

"Well, then, it's most likely to be true, isn't it?"

"Why's that?" I asked.

"No man that big would ever admit to taking tap-dance lessons *unless* he was a suspect in a murder case, now would he?"

"Probably not. Anyway, it will be easy enough to verify. I have a feeling that it's true, too. That means that Grace and I have to strike Murphy's name from our list."

"Why don't we talk more about this while we're eating?" Momma suggested.

"I didn't think I was supposed to discuss my investigations at the dinner table," I said as I followed my mother into the kitchen.

"I'll make an exception just this once,"

Momma said.

She must have had a reason for the exception, but I wasn't going to ask her what it was.

As we started putting food on our plates — chicken, mashed potatoes, green beans, and homemade sourdough bread — Momma asked, "How many suspects does that leave on your list?"

"What makes you think we have a list?" I asked.

"Suzanne, I know you well enough to realize that you're too organized *not* to have one."

"It's true," I admitted. "We still have Rebecca Link from April Springs, and from Pinerush there's Anne Pinerush and her son, Forrest."

"Is that all?" she asked.

"No, there's also a mysterious male cousin somewhere in the background, but no one admits to knowing anything about him."

Momma nodded as she took a bite, and I grabbed my own opportunity to eat some as well. It was wonderful, but it was missing something. "Do we have any cranberries left from before?"

"Why do you ask?"

"I just love canned cranberry jelly with this meal."

"I knew that, but it completely slipped my mind. Let me check," she said as she started to get up, but I rejected the idea and stood myself. "Sit and eat. I'll look."

Momma clearly wasn't pleased with that solution, but I wasn't going to back down. I didn't do enough to keep our household running, so quite literally, it was the least that I could do. I found a can near the back of the fridge. I cut the jelly into inch-and-half servings and laid it out on a fancy plate.

As I came out of the kitchen, I set the plate down. "Isn't it beautiful? It's just something I whipped up," I said with a smile.

"I'm sure it will be delightful," Momma said. After she took some for herself, she asked, "How did our James manage to get himself involved with the Pinerushes?"

"Do you know them?" I asked. It wouldn't have surprised me one bit if she did. Sometimes I felt as though my mother had more connections in North Carolina than Duke Power.

"I know *of* them," she said.

"To be honest with you, I wasn't all that sure about Anne the first time we met, but she was a different woman today." I looked over to see Momma's fork hovering an inch from her mouth. "Are you all right?"

"Am I to understand that you know Anne Pinerush personally?"

"I do," I admitted. "As a matter of fact, Grace and I had an early dinner at the manor this afternoon."

"We'll get to why you were invited in a moment, but am I to understand that this is your second dinner today?"

"It was early, and I'm hungry again."

She started to reach for my plate when I said, "Try to take that at your own risk." I was grinning as I said it, and Momma smiled in return.

"Don't feel as though you have to eat again on my account."

I stuck out my hand toward her. "Hi, I'm your daughter, Suzanne. It's nice to meet you. Have you ever known me to eat anything strictly out of a sense of obligation?"

She laughed at that. "Of course not. So, what was the manor like?"

I described the home, the grounds, and the meal to her, and if I didn't know better, I would have said that my mother was a little starstruck. I hadn't heard much about the Pinerushes at all before James's connection with them, but since then, I knew way too much about them.

"Now for the most important question of all. How did you happen to meet her in the first place?"

"James Settle's last name was really Pinerush," I said. "It turns out that he was one of the heirs to the Pinerush fortune."

Momma took that in, and then nodded. "I'm sure that adds a few suspects to your list. It has been my experience that people kill for one of two reasons: money or love. Rebecca covers the love aspect, and now money covers the rest. So, with James out of the way, am I correct in assuming that his share is divided up among the other two?"

"Three," I said. "Don't forget, there's a cousin nobody talks about who is involved as well."

"What's his name? Is he another Pinerush?"

"I honestly don't know anything else about him," I admitted.

"So, he may or may not be a factor. Are there any other wild cards in the mix?"

"Why are you so curious about this all of a sudden?" I asked. "It's not as though you've cared all that much about the murders I've investigated in the past."

"Let's just say that it involves both my daughter and my paramour and leave it at that. Why wouldn't I be interested?"

"Don't call him that," I said. "It sounds creepy."

" 'Boyfriend' is even worse, though. I suppose I could call him something more intimate if you'd like," I started to cringe when she finished, "perhaps Phillip?"

"Call him whatever you want to," I said. "Just don't call him anything in front of me."

We finished eating, and as we were cleaning up, my cell rang. It was Grace, so I asked Momma, "Do you mind if I get it? It might be important."

"Go on, take it in the living room," she said.

"Don't do all those dishes without me," I said as I flipped open the phone and walked out of the room.

"How did it go, Grace?"

"Murphy is officially off the chief's list of suspects."

"He got confirmation of the class?"

"He did," Grace said.

"Are you home now?" I asked her.

She hesitated, and then said, "Actually, I decided to go out for a while."

"With Murphy?" I asked jokingly.

"As a matter of fact, yes," she answered mildly, as though she was expecting some kind of reaction from me.

"Have fun, then, and don't stay out too late," I said.

"What? No cracks, comments, or laughter?" she asked.

"Hey, you're a grown woman. If you think you can find happiness with a blacksmith, you shouldn't deprive yourself of the chance."

"It's one drink, Suzanne," she said. "It's hardly a proposal."

"You know what Momma used to tell us when we were teenagers," I reminded Grace.

"Don't date anyone you can't see yourself marrying someday," she quoted. "After all, who knows where that first date could lead?"

"Excellent. You get a gold star," I said. "Seriously, have fun. Will you be by the shop tomorrow? You're still off, right?"

"I'll be there," she said. "See you around eleven-fifteen."

"Bye," I said, and then rejoined Momma in the kitchen.

Of course the dishes were finished and drying in the rack by the sink by the time I got there.

"I thought you were going to wait for me," I said.

"You offered, I declined," Momma said

with a smile. "I probably shouldn't even tell you this, but I made a pie today, and it's in the fridge right now."

"Is it cherry?" I asked.

"Apple," she replied.

"With a Dutch crumb topping?"

"Would I make it any other way with you here?" Momma asked with a grin.

"You know what? I could probably make room for a sliver," I admitted.

"I'll join you," she said. We dished up two slices that were both considerably more than slivers, and then took them out into the living room.

As we ate, Momma said, "This is nice. I miss it sometimes."

"What are you talking about? We have pie all of the time," I said.

"I meant a quiet evening with just the two of us here," she said. "What with Jake, Grace, and Phillip, there never seems to be enough time for just us."

I touched her hand lightly as I said, "I know what you mean. We need to both make more of an effort to spend some time together. What should we do, have a date night every week?" I asked with a grin.

"I would agree, but I know that one of us would find a way of breaking it soon enough. Let's just not let these moments slip away from us when they present themselves. We'll take the opportunities as they come and be glad for each and every one of them. Deal?"

"Deal," I said, and then I took another bite of pie. It was delicious cold, and I'd recently decided that I liked it chilled better than when it came hot out of the oven. The juices had a way of growing richer and sweeter if I could only keep from eating the pie the moment it first emerged. I had to admit that it *had* helped that I hadn't been at home when Momma had made it.

I yawned after I took the last bite, and Momma said, "You must be exhausted, and you have to get up earlier than any woman should."

"I'm okay," I said. "What are you reading right now? Is it another mystery?"

"No, I guessed the last three killers correctly, so I'm going to switch to biographies for a while until my keen detective sense isn't so finely honed."

I laughed at that, and then admitted, "I'm glad you can figure out who the killers are. I always think I know, and then it turns out that I guessed wrong. I don't know how the writers do it, do you?"

"It must help knowing who the murderer is ahead of time," she said.

"That's not what Elizabeth from my book club says," I admitted. "She's written to just about all of her favorite authors, and most of them have no clue who the killer is until they get to the very end."

"How can they write like that, not knowing how it's going to turn out?" Momma asked.

"She told us that one of her favorite authors once said that if he doesn't know who did it until the very end, there's not much chance that his readers will be able to guess the identity of the murderer."

"It sounds rather risky if you ask me."

"I couldn't agree with you more," I said. "But Elizabeth has a theory about that as well."

"I can't wait to hear it," Momma said.

"She says it's simple. They all have to be crazy to want to be writers in the first place, so a little more madness is just par for the course."

CHAPTER 14

"Hello, sunshine," I said to Emma the next morning when she came into Donut Heart's kitchen. "You look as though you didn't get enough sleep."

"I didn't," she answered with a grin, "but it was worth it."

"Is there by any chance a new man in your life?" I asked as I finished mixing a new orange marmalade cake donut I'd been experimenting with recently. So far I hadn't had much success, but I still had hopes for it. I didn't feel as though I was doing my job if I couldn't offer my customers at least one new donut a month. That self-imposed rule had led to some frightful donuts in the past and I hadn't always made my goal, but I'd come up with some really nice donuts over the years under pressure from the time limit, too, so it all worked out in the end.

"How did you know?" Emma asked as she grabbed her apron and tied it around her waist. "Is it that obvious?"

"Just for the folks who know you," I said. "What's his name?"

"I don't want to jinx it," she said. "Do you mind if I don't say just yet?"

"Of course I don't," I said. "I didn't mean to pry."

"Suzanne, it's not like that. It's just that he's a little older than I am, and I'm a little sensitive about it."

I put down the bowl and took her hands in mine. "Emma, I'm not going to judge you by who you date or don't date. If you can find someone who makes you happy, I don't care how old he is. Joy is too hard to find in this life to put age limits on it. Hang on a second. He's not creepy old, is he? When you say older, you mean that he's just older than you."

"What do you consider creepy?" she asked.

"For you? Anywhere in his forties, I would say."

"Oh, he's younger than that," she said.

"Is he in his thirties?" I asked. I still thought that might be a little too old for her, regardless of what I'd just said. Believing in something in generalities was one thing, but this was Emma, a girl I'd known her entire life, and I felt extremely overprotective of her.

She laughed. "Suzanne, stop digging. It's nothing all that serious yet, anyway. We just ran into each other at the library last night by coincidence, and we found ourselves chatting about April Springs. He was very interested in everything I had to say."

"I'm sure he was," I said. And then a thought struck me. "Hang on a second. You're not talking about Rome, are you?"

Emma looked at me and asked, "How could you have possibly known that? I realize that he was in the shop yesterday, but how did you put it together that he was the one I was talking to last night?"

"Call it a lucky guess," I said, remembering how Emma had taken off after him the second I'd released her from work. "Do you really think you two might start dating?"

"Why not? He's handsome, and it was clear after I spent two minutes talking to him that he was smart."

"What exactly did he ask you about when you chatted?"

It was a delicate question, and Emma had every right to refuse to answer me, but I really wanted to know.

"He wanted to know how well I knew James," she admitted. "Do you think that's significant?" She frowned for a moment, and then said, "Of course it is. He's not interested in me, is he? I'm just a kid, and he's a grown man."

"Don't sell yourself short," I said. "I'm sure he was attracted to more than just your mind, as glorious as it is. Just be careful, though."

"Why? Because he's older than I am?"

"That, and because of his real name, too. Did he tell you what it was?"

She looked a bit surprised by the question. "Do you mean it's not really Rome?"

"To his friends it is — I'm sure of it — but he told me that his driver's license says that Romance is his true first name."

"Are you making that up?" Emma asked.

"That's what he told me when he was in the shop yesterday," I said. "I meant what I said, though. We don't really know anything about the man, do we? Just be careful."

"I will. And you know what? I think you're right. I'm pretty sure that he was interested in me romantically. And why shouldn't he be? After all, I'm a catch."

"Easy there, girl. You don't want your expectations to get the better of you."

"Why not? As far as I'm concerned, that's part of the fun in it," Emma said. "Besides, what girl doesn't deserve a handsome and mysterious stranger in her life just once?"

I had to laugh. "Just be careful. I ended up marrying mine, and we both know how that turned out."

"I'm not going to get married, at least not anytime soon," she said. "Now, are we going to make donuts or what?"

"I'm getting ready to drop these now," I said. After Emma was out of the kitchen, I got started. As I swung the dropper and added perfect little round wheels of dough to the hot oil, I couldn't help wondering if Rome was interested in Emma, or the information she had about James?

The next time I saw him, I was going to find out. She was too special, too important to me, to let an older and more experienced man take advantage of her.

And while I was at it, I was going to find out what he was really up to, and why he'd come to April Springs in the first place.

At just before six, the donuts were in the display cases and Emma was in back washing dishes. I started watching the clock, and then I decided to go ahead and open anyway. As I headed for the front door flipping lights on as I went, I saw someone already waiting out front for us to open. It reminded me of an old saying my grandmother was fond of, and she never failed to quote it whenever she thought that it was the least bit appropriate. "Speak of the Devil and he appears," she'd always said, and sure enough, Rome was out front waiting patiently for me to unlock the door after Emma and I had been discussing him so recently.

The only question was whether he was there to see Emma, or ask me more questions about James Settle.

"We were just talking about you this morning," I told Rome as I flipped the sign and let him in. "You made quite an impression on my assistant last night."

"What did Emma tell you?" he asked.

"Only that you two met at the library and that you had a wonderful time together. She's got the dopiest grin on her face you've ever seen."

He looked clearly confused. "Why would she act that way?"

"Do you mean that none of it is true?" I asked.

"No, we had a nice chat, but there was nothing more to it than that. For goodness' sake, she's young enough to be my daughter. Well, I might not be that old, but she could at least be my niece."

"So then you have no intention of asking her out on a date?"

He looked miserable when I'd asked him

the question. "No, ma'am, I surely don't. I'm sorry if she got the wrong impression."

I nodded. "When you tell her, do me a favor and let her down gently, okay? She's a dreamer who still believes in love at first sight."

"I do myself," he admitted. "Just not with someone as young as she is."

"So then, if you aren't here to see Emma, to what do we owe the pleasure of your company? Were you looking for more donuts?"

"Actually, I was hoping that you were able to find out something more about what happened to James Settle," he said.

"As a matter of fact, I have," I admitted. "Why is he suddenly so important to you, though? You said that you didn't even know the man when you came in before."

"No, I didn't," Rome admitted. "But from everything I've heard, I would have liked to meet him very much. Hasn't that ever happened to you? You hear about something random and wonder why it ever happened in the first place."

"There was nothing random about his murder," I said. "It was intentional."

"Listen, I didn't mean to offend you. I'm sincerely interested, though. Would you tell me what you've found out so far?"

"I'm not sure that I should," I said.

"I wouldn't ask if it weren't important to me, though I can't tell you why. Please?"

I was tempted — the man was as slick and smooth as could be — when Emma walked out. "I thought I heard voices out here."

The moment she saw that it was Rome, her face lit up. She was clearly smitten, and I hoped that Rome would let her down gently. "Hey there, stranger. Did you come by just to see me?" she asked him as she ran her fingers through her hair.

"Emma, can we talk?"

Her smile faded. "It's never good when someone says that to you, is it?"

He shrugged. "I don't know what to say. I'm sorry; you are truly a wonderful young woman, and if I were fifteen years younger, I can promise you that you'd have a difficult time getting rid of me." As he said it, he smiled in a way that led me to believe that every word of it was true.

"Don't be that way," Emma said, trying her best to change his mind. "Age is just a number, after all, and we all have to take love where we find it. Can either one of us afford to limit it to numbers?"

Was she honestly quoting me now? This was not good. I hoped Rome had experience with this, because if he allowed her to persuade him that they could be together, she could talk him into anything.

Rome looked at her intently as he said, "Emma, I wish I could say that it was true for me as well, but I'm afraid that it matters to me."

She took it all in, and then sniffed the air a few times. It seemed as though she was fighting back tears, but she got past the moment and said, "I'm really sorry you feel that way, Rome, and if you ever change your mind, you're welcome to come ask me out later, but I'm not at all sure that I'll say yes."

"It is a chance I must regretfully take," he said.

Emma nodded, looked at me briefly, and then went back to her dishes.

Once she was gone, Rome looked at me and said, "I really botched that up, didn't I?"

"Are you kidding? That went spectacularly. You left her with her pride, which is more than I thought you'd ever be able to do. Have you ever let someone down that gently before?"

"No, and I hope I never have to do it again. She just about convinced me that I was wrong after all. Someday I might even regret turning her down."

"I wouldn't blame you if you did." I knew

that it would be crazy to tell this man so much of what I'd discovered, but the tender way he'd handled Emma made me inclined to tell him what he wanted to know. Besides, if I spoke with a complete stranger about the case, it might help me clarify my own thoughts and suspicions. In the end, what harm could it do to share? "Do you still want to know about James and the case?"

"I didn't think you wanted to tell me."

"Let's just say that you convinced me. What do you want to know, and I'll tell you what I can."

"Everything," he said.

"Then let me get you some coffee and a treat and I'll cover what I can."

Ten minutes later, after he'd had a donut and some coffee as I briefed him, Rome was on his way. He thanked me for my time, left an overly generous tip, and then took off.

I waited on a few customers, and then called Emma out front. "Could you come out here for a second?"

She came to the door, but wouldn't walk through. "Is he still here?"

"No, he left a while ago."

"Why did he stay so long?" she asked, clearly a little hurt by my acceptance of him after he'd turned her down.

"He wanted to know more about James,

and I told him. Listen, I'm proud of you for the way you handled that."

"How so?" Emma asked. "I thought I was kind of rude, actually."

"My dear friend, I can say with complete sincerity that you handled it better than I ever could have."

"Do you mean that? I really am trying to grow up."

I hugged her, and then I said, "If you ask me, you already have."

She nodded, and then disappeared back into the kitchen. I didn't know why, but I always felt somewhat maternal toward her, though she had a perfectly fine mother of her own. Still, she was all the work family I had, and we'd formed a bond closer than any employer and employee. When Emma had been gone exploring the world, I'd missed her greatly, and though I hadn't begrudged her the opportunity to get out of April Springs to see what else was out there, no one short of her mother and father had been happier to have her back among us.

I was about to give Lily Hamilton her change when I happened to glance out the window toward the park across the street. Standing near the abandoned railroad tracks — mine according to the document that

James Settle had signed over to me — I saw Rebecca Link looking all around her in anticipation of something happening. Was she waiting for someone there? I kept watching, even though nothing was going on, because I was dying to know who she might be seeing. The next time I glanced her way, I saw something that I didn't like. Was that fear on her face, or was I mistaken?

"Suzanne, what's going on?" Lily asked, bringing me back to my shop.

"I'm sorry, Lily. I zoned out for just a second."

She nodded as she dropped her change into her purse. "Don't worry about it. That happens to me all of the time." Lily was dressed in her EMT outfit, and I hoped that she was exaggerating. She had a vital job to do that I'd assumed took all of her attention, and the idea of her mind wandering was a disturbing one.

"Not on the job, though," she quickly added.

"That's good to hear."

After she started out the front door, I glanced outside again, but Rebecca was gone. "Hey Emma, could you come up here?"

She appeared quickly, and I said, "Take over. I'll be right back." I knew that she wasn't all that fond of working the front, but it couldn't be helped. I grabbed my light jacket and headed outside, putting it on over my apron. As I walked in the direction where I'd last seen Rebecca, I kept scanning the folks around me. The day was much warmer than it had been over the last week, and I was glad for it. Where had Rebecca disappeared to? I looked and looked, but I couldn't find any sign of her anywhere. It was odd to say the least, but I couldn't spend all of my time tracking her down.

I walked over to the Boxcar just in case she'd ducked in there, but I didn't see her sitting at any of the booths.

Much to my surprise though, Forrest Pinerush *was* there, scowling at a copy of the *April Springs Sentinel* as he sipped a cup of coffee.

I nodded to Trish and held a finger to my lips. She nodded back, and I made my way to Forrest's table. He was wearing a suit that looked as though it had been made in some European capital instead of here in North Carolina. His tie alone was probably worth more than my Jeep, and if I had to guess, I figured that his complete ensemble probably exceeded my entire net worth. I didn't like him for several reasons, not the least of which was his choice of flaunting his wealth through his clothing, but the thing I despised most of all was the way he'd treated James.

"What's the matter, Forrest? Did you find something in our little local paper that you don't approve of?" I asked.

He looked up from the newspaper, clearly startled to see me standing there. "Suzanne, what are you doing here? Don't you have a donut shop to run?"

"I'm on my break," I said as I sat in the chair across from him. "Mind if I join you?"

"The question's a little late for you to ask, don't you think?"

"What are you doing here, Forrest?" I asked him.

"Not that it's any of your business, but I have a meeting," he said.

"Is it with Rebecca Link, by any chance?" It was a wild shot, but still one worth taking.

"I don't have the slightest idea who you're talking about. Mother demanded that I meet Thomas Oak here and get his progress report. Why he couldn't come out to the manor is beyond me."

I felt as though it had more to do with the power struggle between mother and son than it did with inconveniencing the attorney, but I wasn't about to say anything.

"Has he made any progress that you know of?"

"If I could answer that, I wouldn't have had to come all the way here for this meeting, now would I?"

"Mind if I sit in, too?" I asked.

"Actually yes, I do mind, very much."

I laughed it off. "That's the way to extend the warm hand of friendship. I'll find out soon enough, since your mother told me that she was going to instruct him to keep me updated as well. If you're not careful, I'm going to tell your mommy on you, Woody."

He visibly flinched at the name, and I knew that I'd scored a direct hit. "No one, and I mean no one, calls me that. Do you understand?"

"Sorry," I said, though I wasn't, not one bit, and what was more, I was certain that he knew it. "James used to refer to you that way, didn't he?"

"It was an annoying childhood habit of his that I thought he'd outgrown a long time ago. Did you hear it from him?"

"Indirectly," I said, trying not to give too much away. I was on a fishing expedition, so it wouldn't hurt my cause if Forrest thought I knew more than I actually did.

"I was under the impression that he didn't

mention his family to anyone."

"We were friends," I said. "We chatted about a great many things." Both of those statements were true, but combined, they turned into one big lie. It was a rather elegant way of bending the truth, if I had to say so myself.

"Well, now that you've learned it, you can promptly forget it. I've grown a great deal since my childhood. What else did he tell you about me?"

It was too good an opportunity to pass up. I decided to take a shot at him squarely between the eyes. "Are you asking me if he told me about you having him committed to an insane asylum?"

"It was a mental health facility," he said. "I was concerned about his well-being, and no one else would take action."

"Could that be because your mother was sick in bed at the time?" I asked.

He started to stand, so I quickly added, "Did I hit a little too close to home just then? Where are you going? I thought you had a meeting."

"We can hold it elsewhere," he snapped. "Someplace that's more private and less apt to interruption would be nice."

As he stormed out, he threw a fifty at Trish and grumbled, "Keep the change."

I approached her and said, "Sorry about that. I didn't mean to run any of your customers off."

She held the fifty up to the light, nodded in approval, and then put it into her till. "With that kind of tip, you can hose them down with the fire extinguisher if you'd like. Why was he so upset, anyway?"

"You don't know who that was, do you?" I asked softly.

"I sure don't. Why do you ask? Should I?" she asked, looking puzzled by my question.

"That was James's cousin, Forrest."

Trish's expression turned to sheer hatred as she started for the door.

I stepped in her way, effectively blocking her path. "Hang on a second. You need to think about what you're about to do."

"Get out of my way, Suzanne. That man had James locked up," Trish snapped. "He's not going to get away with it."

"Let me ask you something first. Did James attack him when he had the chance?" I asked.

"No, he said he just wanted to forget that it had ever happened."

"So didn't he have more of a right to be angry than you are right now?"

That managed to calm her down. "No, but that man is the reason that James left his old life behind."

"As bad as it was," I said, "isn't that the reason he ended up here in April Springs, and eventually to you? I'm not trying to justify what Forrest did to him, and I'm certainly not making excuses for the man, but what good would it do for you to go after him now?"

"I don't know. I might feel better if I slapped his face a few times," she said, the tension beginning to ease somewhat.

"Maybe for a few seconds, but the man probably has more attorneys on his staff than you have chairs in the diner. You can't win if you go after him like that."

"Suzanne, since when have *you* ever backed off from a fight?" Trish asked.

"If the cause is doomed from the start, it doesn't mean that I'll give up on it, but I always try to take the time to think it through before I do anything rash. I learned that lesson the hard way."

"How so?" she asked.

"Remember when I flew off the handle with Lester Moorefield? The next day he was dead, and I was the main suspect."

"Are you saying that you shouldn't have gone after him?" Trish asked.

"Logically, that's exactly what I'm saying."

"But emotionally?" she asked.

"Yeah, he deserved the grief I gave him. If you want to risk losing the diner in a lawsuit, go ahead. I'll even hold his arms for you."

I stepped aside, and as I did, Trish dropped her head a little. "I just hate it when you're right," she said as she smiled at me.

"It can be really annoying, can't it? Momma does it to me all of the time."

"I might not go after him physically, but if he ever shows his face again, I'm going to lace his sweet tea with ipecac."

"How's that going to reflect on your diner if he stumbles out of here throwing up?" I asked.

"Okay, maybe not that, but how about some strong laxatives in his fudge brownies?"

"Why don't you just give him a dirty look," I suggested. "You have some monstrous scowls that scare me."

She hugged me, and then tweaked one of my ears.

"What was that for?"

"The hug, or the flick?"

"Either. I guess I mean both."

Trish smiled as she said, "The hug was for stopping me from making a big mistake."

"And the ear tweak?"

"The same reason, actually."

I shook my head as I laughed. "I'd love to stay and chat, but I have a donut shop to run across the street."

"I was wondering about that," Trish said with a smile.

I found Forrest ten feet from the diner, clearly waiting impatiently for Thomas Oak.

As I approached him, he said in a bit of a huff, "I'm not interested in discussing anything more with you, Suzanne."

"That's good. You don't have to say a word; all you have to do is listen. I wouldn't go back in there if I were you. It's some free advice, and I'd follow it."

"Why should I?"

"The owner was dating James when he was murdered," I said. "And I just told her that you were the one who had him locked up against his will."

Forrest's face reddened, and he was about to say something when Thomas Oak appeared. He was dressed nicely, though not as stylishly as his client, and he held a battered old leather briefcase that looked somehow out of place with the rest of his attire. "Forrest, whatever you're about to say, I suggest that you keep it to yourself."

"Who are you trying to protect, Oak?" he asked.

"At the moment, you."

"Let's get this meeting over with," Forrest said, "so I can get out of this dump of a town and head back to civilization."

"Why don't you wait for me over there?" he suggested as he pointed to a nearby bench.

"Why should I?" Forrest asked angrily.

"Because your mother asked me to handle this, and I'm doing my best to do just that. I suggest that if you have a problem with that, you take it up with her."

There was a moment when I thought Forrest was going to ignore the attorney, but after a short pause, he walked to the bench as he was told, acting like a sullen four-year-old the whole way.

"That was excellent," I said with a grin to the attorney. "Can you make him do tricks, too? I'd love to see him try to do a handstand."

"I'm doing my best not to press my luck," Oak said. "Are you free around eleven this morning? I need to speak with you."

"That depends. What's our topic of conversation?"

"Mrs. Pinerush has instructed me to tell you everything I've learned in the investigation so far. It's the same information I'm about to deliver to Forrest."

"Why don't I just hang around so you don't have to go to the trouble of saying everything twice?" I asked.

He suppressed a grin as he said, "As tempting as that sounds, we'd better follow Mrs. Pinerush's instructions to the letter."

"Coward," I said with a smile.

"You'd better believe it. Every chance I get."

"I'll see you soon, then," I said. As a last jibe, I leaned past him and waved to Forrest. "Always a pleasure seeing you, Forrie."

He sneered in my direction, a victory in my mind, so I left him there on the bench and went back to Donut Hearts. I wondered what Thomas Oak had uncovered in his own investigation, and if he might have discovered something that Grace and I had missed.

It was all I could do to wait until he had time for me.

MIXED AND MATCHED

I use store-bought mixes sometimes when I'm too tired to do much else in the donut department. They rarely let you down, and you can do some cool combinations with them as well. This recipe uses a buttermilk biscuit mix as a base, but you can see that I've really ramped it up.

Ingredients

Mixed
- 1 egg, lightly beaten
- 1/2 cup sour cream
- 1/4 cup sugar, white granulated
- 1 tablespoon buttermilk
- 1 teaspoon vanilla extract

Sifted
- 1 1/2 cups biscuit mix (we like Jiffy)
- 1/2 teaspoon cinnamon
- 1/2 teaspoon nutmeg
- Dash of salt

- Canola oil for frying (the amount depends on your pot or fryer)

Instructions
In one bowl, beat the egg lightly, and then add the sour cream, sugar, buttermilk, and

vanilla extract. In a separate bowl, sift together the biscuit mix, cinnamon, nutmeg, and salt.

Add the dry ingredients to the wet, mixing well until you have a smooth consistency.

Drop bits of dough using a small-sized cookie scoop (the size of your thumb, approximately). Fry in hot canola oil (360 to 370 degrees F) 1 1/2 to 2 minutes, turning halfway through.

Yield: 10–12 donut drops

CHAPTER 15

The attorney was as good as his word, showing up on the donut shop's doorstep just as I was about to lock up for the day. I let him inside, and then bolted the door behind him.

"Thank you for your patience," he said. "It is much appreciated." His gaze went behind me as he asked, "Is there any possibility that I could get a cup of coffee? I'd be happy to pay for it."

"Sure, but it'll be ten dollars, seeing how you're some hotshot lawyer from the big city," I answered as I poured him a cup.

"Charge me a hundred if you'd like. It's just going on my expense account anyway."

"You're no fun at all," I said. "In that case, it's on the house."

"Then you might throw in one of those apple fritters as well, if you don't mind. I skipped breakfast, and I have a feeling that my lunch is going to be delayed as well."

I did as he asked, and found the man pretty personable when he wasn't trying to manipulate me with his client's money.

"How do you do it?" I asked as I freshened up his coffee.

"Do what?" he asked after taking a sip.

"Turn your charm off and on like that. When you were here the last time, I was ready to throw you out on your ear, but right now, you seem like a pretty decent guy to me."

"I am," he explained after taking a bite of fritter. "Just don't tell anyone. It would ruin my reputation. It's just that I have to act differently sometimes, depending on my role at the time."

"All I know is that I couldn't do it," I said. "With me, it's pretty much a case of what you see is what you get."

"I hope you don't hold our previous interaction against me," he said.

"I'll try not to. Anne said you were going to come by to brief me, so I've been expecting you."

"Do you honestly call her Anne to her face?" he asked, clearly curious about our sudden relationship.

"She asked me to, and I agreed. Why shouldn't I? After all, she calls me Suzanne."

He looked impressed as he explained, "It's

just that there aren't many people on a first-name basis with Mrs. Pinerush."

"What can I say," I said as I started cleaning up. "I must be special."

"You must be."

At that moment, Emma came up front. "Everything's finished in back." Then she spotted Thomas Oak. "I'm sorry, I thought we were closed."

"We are," I said. "The good news is that you get to go home early today."

"I don't mind hanging around."

"Emma, you know how rare the opportunity comes for you to skip out ahead of time, even though you got to go early yesterday. Do you really want to forgo the honor just to hang around with me?"

She shrugged after a second. "What can I say, Suzanne? When you're right, you're right." As she took off her apron, she neared me and whispered, "Is everything okay here?"

"Don't worry; I'm perfectly safe with Thomas Oak. The attorney from Pinerush is here to talk to me about James Settle's murder."

She nodded, and then left after ditching her apron and grabbing her purse.

"That was clever of you," Oak said after Emma was gone. "You managed to mention my name, occupation, and home location all in the same sentence. Your assistant knows everything she needs to about me in case something happens to you. You aren't worried that I'm some kind of threat, are you?"

"Not physically," I said. "You might sue me, but I doubt you'd try to attack me. If you did, I can promise you that you'd find yourself on the short end of a nasty surprise." I was close enough to my baseball bat to grab it and swing it hard before he could get up from his seat. I'd leave the fancy weapons to Angelica; I was more of a Louisville Slugger gal myself.

"Let me assure you that you're safe in either instance," he said. After he finished his fritter, he sipped the last of his coffee. "That was wonderful. You're quite talented, aren't you?"

"I have my moments. As much as I'd love to hang around here and chat with you, can we get started? I've got a meeting myself soon."

"With Grace Gauge, I believe," he said, "your partner in crime."

"More like my co-investigator," I said, "but yes, she's coming by."

"There are no worries about time, since what I have to convey to you can be done rather briefly. The two things that I am about to tell you are not public knowledge, and Mrs. Pinerush has asked me to express her appreciation in advance if you would keep all of this information private."

"I'll tell Grace, my mother, and my boyfriend, regardless of what it is. After that, I'd have to say that it all depends," I said.

"On what?"

"I have three questions for you. Is it criminal for me to know it, does it hurt anyone if I don't tell it, and will I get in trouble with the police chief if I keep it to myself?"

"None of those conditions apply," he said.

"Okay then, you have my word."

"Good," he said as he nodded. "First things first, then. I'm sorry to have to say this, but she thought it was important that you know. Mrs. Pinerush is dying."

I couldn't believe it! I knew that she was older, but she'd been healthy enough when I'd seen her last. "What's wrong with her?"

"I haven't been told myself. She could live another eighteen months, or she could die tomorrow."

"Isn't that true of all of us?" I asked. "There are no guarantees in life."

"While that's technically true, her doctors will be amazed if she makes it past two years, and I have a feeling that you'll live well beyond that."

"Why tell me?" I asked. "It's not like we're that close. We just met."

"She has a favor to ask of you, and it's pertinent. Mrs. Pinerush said there was something that you can do that will give her great comfort in her final moments."

"Of course. If it's in my power, I'll do it."

"Find James's killer before she dies," he said simply.

"I'm trying, but I can't make any promises. I'm just an amateur, after all. She could afford an army of private investigators, all of them ex-cops. Why should she depend on me? Honestly, I'm not at all sure that I like that kind of pressure."

"Mrs. Pinerush has consulted with several people she trusts, and she's been assured that bringing in outsiders is the worst thing she can do at this stage. This case will most likely be solved by the police, but if anyone else has a chance, Mrs. Pinerush firmly believes that it is you and your friends."

"I wish I had that kind of faith in our detecting abilities," I said.

"Her confidence is not without merit. I've investigated your past, and I know that you've been successful before in unmasking murderers."

I didn't know how to respond. "What can I say? I had a lot of help from my friends."

"There's more to it than that," he said. "So, may I tell her that you'll redouble your efforts and do your utmost to find James's killer as soon as possible?"

"You may, and thank her for the faith she's putting in me, no matter how misplaced I think it might be."

He grinned slightly at that before he stifled it. "I will."

"What's the second thing?" I asked. "You said there were two items on the agenda."

"I did indeed. The second item is in regard to her nephew."

"What about James?"

"Not him. Her *other* nephew."

"The mysterious stranger that no one seems to know anything about?" I asked.

"I'm afraid we haven't been completely forthcoming with some information, and Mrs. Pinerush believes that withholding it from you now would be a disservice to your cause."

"By all means, tell me what you can about him."

"I can do better than that," he said as he reached into his briefcase. He withdrew a photograph and slid it across the counter toward me.

The second I saw it, I felt my breath escape. In my heart I'd known it all along. The photograph was just a confirmation of what my subconscious had already figured out.

It was Rome, the new man who had just showed up in April Springs. I'd realized early on that it was more than a coincidence that he'd been digging into James Settle's murder himself.

And why shouldn't he?

After all, they were cousins, weren't they?

"Is he a suspect in Anne's mind?" I asked after I took a moment to collect myself. I had done my best not to give away the fact that I already knew the man. It was a card I might need later, so there was no reason to play it just yet.

"Rome? No, there's not a chance of that."

"How can you both be so sure?"

Mr. Oak smiled softly. "Mainly because he and James had the same idea about distributing their wealth. You see, they both tried to turn down the family fortune. Rome just went about it differently."

"What did he do?" I asked.

"Instead of giving it all away, he's been using the interest and dividends to help people here at home, and all over the world as well. When he learned that he couldn't touch the principal, he found a clever way to get his hands on the rest of it, and the only thing he's done since then is to try his best to make the world a better place."

"You probably think he's crazy for doing it, don't you?" I asked.

"Actually, I admire him. After all, I'm the one who helped him free up the money that he's using for good."

That put the attorney in a new light. Maybe he wasn't the bad guy I'd initially believed he was. "So, aren't you kind of exposing him now by telling me?"

"Mrs. Pinerush isn't a supporter of Rome's philosophy any more than she was of James's ideals, but I believe that she always secretly felt that both of them were men of action who should be respected, instead of idlers who talked but never really did anything."

"Like her son?" I asked.

There was the flash of a quick grin, killed with great speed. "We were discussing Rome, I believe. If he comes to April Springs, you should trust him."

I considered telling Mr. Oak that Rome was already here, but I decided that I was under no obligation to do so. What reason did I have to tell him? I was beginning to like him, but that didn't mean that I had to tell him everything that I knew.

"If it's appropriate, then I will," I said.

A sudden knock on the front door startled me, and I looked up to see Grace standing there, a curious expression on her face as she watched me through the glass.

"Was there anything else?" I asked as I started for the door.

"No, that concludes our business," he answered as he slipped the photograph back into his briefcase.

As I unlocked the door for Grace, he handed me his card and said, "If you need anything that Mrs. Pinerush might be able to provide, all you have to do is call."

"Wow, that's some kind of magic wish, isn't it?"

"That's the business I'm in," he said.

He nodded to Grace, and then left the donut shop.

"What was that all about?"

"Boy, do I have a lot to tell you." Though I'd agreed to keep Mrs. Pinerush's secrets, I'd also warned the attorney that there was no way I was going to exclude Grace or Jake or my mother. They could be all trusted, and I knew that there was no way Momma would disregard my request if I asked her to keep quiet about it. Her relationship with the police chief was important to her, I knew that, but it still wasn't as significant as the one we had.

Grace was just as surprised as I was about Mrs. Pinerush's condition, and Rome's true identity.

After I'd brought her up to date, Grace said, "It's all kind of hard to believe, isn't it?"

"There's no reason to lie about any of it," I said.

"So, that means that we can eliminate two of our suspects from the list," Grace said. "We have to trust that Rome didn't have any reason to wish James harm, and we already know that Murphy didn't do it."

"How is he, by the way?" I asked Grace with a hint of a grin.

"How should I know?" she asked.

"You're the one who saw him last," I said. "I was just curious. What did you two end up doing last night?"

"We spent some time chatting, and then we said good night, and I went home. Alone."

It sounded as though I might have gone a little too far in teasing her. "Hey, I'm sorry. I didn't mean anything by it."

"No, you're fine. I'm most likely just a little touchy about spending time with him. I still feel like I'm robbing the cradle by even considering going out with him on a date. He's Spencer's little brother, for goodness' sake."

"Grace, he's two years younger than we are, and we aren't exactly fresh produce."

"Are you saying that we're heading for the compost pile?" she asked me with a grin.

"Well, maybe not yet."

"That's good to know."

"So, did he ask you out?" I asked.

"As a matter of fact, he did."

"And you turned him down?"

"No, not quite," she admitted. "I told him that I'd have to think about it."

"How did he react to that?" I asked.

"He said he'd already waited all of these years to get up the courage to ask me, so it was only fair that I took my time answering him."

"That sounds reasonable," I said. "What are you going to do?"

"I have no idea. Can we talk about something else, maybe something less personal?"

"How about if we figure out what to do next in our investigation?" I offered.

"That sounds like an excellent idea to me," Grace said. "So, as far as we can figure it, we have two main suspects left: Forrest Pinerush and Rebecca Link."

"We had five, we eliminated two, and now

we have two left. I wasn't a math major in college, but that doesn't add up," I said.

"I just assumed that we'd strike Anne's name as well," Grace said. "If she had it done herself, she wouldn't be pleading with you to solve the murder, now would she?"

"It's highly doubtful," I agreed. "So then, we have two suspects — and neither of them is all that fond of us — and now we have to grill them until one of them cracks. Is that the plan?"

"It works for me," she said. "Which one should we start with?"

"Well, considering that I've already antagonized Forrest quite a bit today, I think we should find Rebecca and push her a little harder." I told her what I'd seen through the window, and Grace agreed that it warranted another session of questioning.

"Let's go," Grace said as she headed for the door.

"One thing, though," I said. "I still have to finish the dishes, sweep the floors, run the report on my cash register, and then make my deposit."

"I don't know why your business has to interfere so much with our investigations," Grace said with a smile. "After all, mine doesn't."

"No disrespect intended, but mine would

326

fall apart without me."

"And you don't think that mine would?" she asked casually.

"In the long run? Absolutely. Day to day? We've proven that's not the case time and time again, haven't we?"

"Oh, yes," she said with a laugh. "That's one of the things I love so much about my job. I won't do your dishes, but I don't mind sweeping up and wiping the tables down."

"Hey, I'll take whatever I can get," I said as I started running the report on my register. "I for one am thrilled that you have a job you can ignore so you can help me."

"Hey, my boss ordered me to take the week off, remember? Believe me, I enjoy sleuthing, too. I just hope we can figure out which one of our suspects killed James. I wonder if Chief Martin has narrowed it down that far as well."

"For all I know, he has a completely different list of suspects than we do," I admitted.

"Honestly, I don't care who catches the killer," Grace said. "I just want whoever did it to pay for what they did."

"I couldn't agree with you more."

With the place cleaned up and the report balanced, I looked around for my deposit slips, and then realized that I'd left them in the Jeep. I wasn't worried about anyone stealing one. If they did, what could they do, deposit more money in my anemic account? It wasn't like I was carrying a ton of money in it anyway, since I'd just paid off my suppliers. Whatever was left an industrious thief was more than welcome to.

As I locked up, I said, "We need to take the Jeep."

"Why not ride in style?" Grace asked. "You've driven my car. Wouldn't you rather go in something that has actual windows?"

"Hey, my Jeep has windows."

"I mean ones made of glass and not plastic," she replied.

"That's a point. Let me just grab something from the glove box and we'll go track Rebecca down."

When I got close to the Jeep, I realized that something was wrong. Someone had gotten in and unzipped my windows. Now, who would do that? And then I saw that they hadn't been unzipped at all.

The vandal had taken a knife and cut the plastic out of the flimsy frames. It wasn't much as far as destruction went, but it was enough to get my attention.

"Who would do something like this?" I asked as I surveyed the damage.

"Juvenile delinquents most likely," Grace answered. "The chief needs to do something about them."

I looked at the windows a little closer and wondered if they could be repaired. No, whoever had slashed them had done a pretty thorough job of it. But was this really a random act of violence, or had it been meant as a message to me to back off?

"Grace, how do we know this isn't a warning from the killer?"

"Well, for one thing, there's no note, and as for scaring you, they could have done much worse. It was most likely just crazy kids, but if you want to call Chief Martin and report it, go right ahead."

I thought about it, and then rejected the idea. If Grace assumed that it was just vandalism, what chance did I have of convincing the police that it had been intended to scare me? Then again, I couldn't just let it go. Maybe there was someone else I could ask.

I took out my cell phone and called the mayor. "George, this is Suzanne. Do you have a second?"

"For you, always. How are you doing?" he asked. "It's good to hear from you. There's nothing wrong, is there?"

"Why do you ask that?"

"Well, you usually don't call me in the middle of the day for no reason. Did something happen?"

"To be honest, someone just slashed the windows on my Jeep."

"They got yours, too?" he asked.

"Did someone else's car get targeted?"

"Someone cut Eric Thompson's rear window out of his Triumph TR-3 about an hour ago. I just overheard Chief Martin on the phone with him. He was in my office updating me on the investigation when the call came in."

I suddenly didn't care about my car windows anymore. "Did he have anything interesting to tell you?"

"I wish I could tell you everything that he just told me, but it's not something I can discuss with you," he said. "The chief has to know that whatever he tells me is kept in the strictest confidence, or he's not going to be forthcoming with me in the future."

"I understand. Not even a hint, though?"

"Sorry," he said with a laugh. "This job's not all it's cracked up to be if I can't even help my friends."

"You're helping me plenty just by being our mayor," I said. "As far as I'm concerned, it's a small price to pay."

"Maybe so, but I'm not having nearly as

much fun as I used to when working with you on a case. Then again, I didn't exactly ask for this job, did I?" George had been the victim of a write-in campaign orchestrated by my mother.

"I didn't have anything to do with that, remember?"

"I know full well who to blame," he said with a laugh. "Good luck in your hunt, and I'm sorry about your windows. The chief's otherwise occupied at the moment, but I'll make sure that he or one of his men come look at it."

"It's parked near the donut shop. I'm going to be riding around with Grace this afternoon, so it will be there all day."

"Happy hunting, and you two be careful."

"We always are," I said, and then hung up.

"Someone else got hit?" Grace asked me the second I put my phone away.

"A Triumph. It appears that there's a crime spree in town."

Grace smiled as I said it, so I asked, "Why the grin?"

"It wasn't a warning. That's a good thing, right?"

"I don't know. It might mean that we're so far from catching the killer that we don't even pose a threat to them."

"We're crafty, though," Grace said. "They won't know they're caught until the chief puts the handcuffs on them."

"I just hope we figure it all out before they do," I said.

"Do you still have the heart to go after Rebecca?"

"Now more than ever," I said.

"Then let's get my car and see if we can track her down."

CHAPTER 16

It wasn't to be, though. Rebecca had skipped her shift at the convenience store again, and she wasn't at her apartment, either. Where could she be? Was there a chance she was on the run, thinking that someone might be close to catching her?

I suddenly had a more ominous thought. It was clear that she'd been meeting someone in the park that morning. From the brief look at her face, I hadn't seen a killer in her eyes. Instead, there had been fear, and maybe even panic. What if Grace and I had gotten it wrong from the very start? Just suppose Rebecca was a potential victim, and not the killer? It changed the entire way we'd been looking at her.

"I've got a crazy idea," I told Grace. "What if we're jumping to conclusions here about Rebecca's viability as a suspect?"

"Anything's possible. I'm willing to listen to whatever you have to say," Grace said as she pulled over and parked so she could focus on our conversation.

"What if Rebecca is another potential victim instead of the possible murderer?"

Grace's eyebrows both shot up. "That's a pretty big jump, Suzanne. Do you have anything to back it up?"

"When I saw her out in the park waiting for someone today, she seemed scared to death to me, as though she wasn't looking forward to the conversation that she was about to have. Could the killer have lured her there in order to duplicate his crime? What kind of irony would it be if Rebecca was killed near where James was murdered?"

"I don't know," Grace said. "What could the motive be that would cover both James and Rebecca?"

"I'm not sure. Maybe I'm just jumping at shadows, but what if James wasn't killed because of his family money *or* a romance that went bad? What if he saw something he wasn't supposed to see, or he knew something that he wasn't supposed to know? He could have been killed to keep him quiet."

"Even if that's true, then why kill Rebecca as well?"

"She and James were a couple, and not so long ago. He could have told her about what he knew without realizing that he was putting her in jeopardy, and that's why the murderer might be after her, too." Something darker just occurred to me. "Grace, if that's true, then Trish could be in trouble as well. James could have told her whatever he told Rebecca. Drive to the Boxcar as fast as you can."

"You realize that we're both panicking based on very little solid proof," Grace said as she started her car and took off.

"Maybe so, but wouldn't you rather take the chance of looking a little silly and being sure that Trish is okay, rather than finding out later that we could have stopped something bad from happening but we didn't do anything because we were afraid we might look foolish if we were wrong?"

"I'd take that chance every time," she said as she sped toward the diner. Fortunately we weren't that far away.

When we got there, though, I became more upset than ever.

For the first time in recent memory, there was a sign on Trish's restaurant, and the dining room inside was dark.

All it said was CLOSED, and I couldn't help wondering if something might have already happened to Trish.

■ ■ ■ ■

I dialed her private number, but it went straight to voice mail. "She's not answering," I said, the sense of panic rising in me.

"Did you try her personal line?"

"That's the one I just called," I said. "Grace, I'm worried."

"It's not time to panic yet. Let's go."

"Where are we headed?"

"We're going out to her place on the lake. If she's not here, she's bound to be there, wouldn't you think?"

"I hope you're right," I said. I kept trying her number as Grace drove, but the result was always the same.

"Did you try the restaurant, just in case she left a message on the machine?" Grace asked me when we were halfway to Trish's house.

"No, I thought the sign said it all."

"See if she left anything on the recording."

I did as Grace asked, but there was no answer, and more importantly, no message, either. "This is crazy. There's always a message on her Boxcar number about the day's specials."

"Maybe they decided not to do one since

they weren't going to be open today. It's not necessarily a bad thing, Suzanne."

"It's not good, either," I said. As we drove on, my sense of dread began to increase exponentially. What if something had already happened to Trish? Had Grace and I missed a significant clue that could have saved her? I knew our investigations were serious business, but it was becoming too real to me at the moment. Trish was nearly as important to me as Grace and Momma were. If something had happened to her, especially something that I might have been able to stop if I'd just been clever enough, I didn't know how I would ever be able to live with myself.

As we pulled up to Trish's house, we both saw that her car wasn't parked out front.

"She's not here," Grace said, her voice full of defeat.

"Maybe she parked in the garage," I said, desperate and hopeful at the same time.

"Suzanne, has she ever done that as long as you've known her?" Grace asked me.

"Maybe once or twice. Come on. Let's check it out."

There was no window in the garage, and when I tested the door, it was locked. The windows of the house were blocked off from light as well, with the shades drawn all around.

"That just leaves the deck," Grace said.

We walked around the house, and I found myself hoping beyond hope that we'd see Trish curled up on one of the deck chairs.

No one was there, though.

"Where could she be?" I asked.

"I don't know. Is there anyone we can even call at this point? Do you have the numbers for the women who work with her at the diner?"

"No, I never needed them before. I'm not even certain that I know their last names. It's just one big dead end."

"What should we do, then?" Grace asked me.

"There's only one thing we can do. We weren't able to find Trish, but maybe we can still save Rebecca. We need to find her, and fast, and try to find out who she was meeting in the park," I replied. "It might be the only clue we get to saving either one of them."

"Where can we look for her? She's not at work; we know that much."

"Then we need to find out where she is," I said. "Go straight to the police station. I'm sure that once we explain everything, Chief Martin will help us track her down.

Who knows? He might even be able to help us find Trish, too."

We never made it to the station, though. I got a call instead that changed everything from that point forward.

The second my cell phone rang, I looked at the caller ID, hoping against hope that it was Trish.

It was no surprise then that I couldn't keep the disappointment out of my voice when I saw that it was Jake.

"Hey there," I said. "What's up?"

"Suzanne, what's wrong? Did something happen?"

"No. Yes. I don't know," I replied, trying my best to hide my emotions from him.

"That certainly clears it all up. Take a deep breath, and then tell me what's going on."

I did, relaying Rebecca's expressions in the park and Trish's sudden disappearance. "Have you called Chief Martin yet?" he asked as soon as I finished.

"We're heading over to the police station right now, but I'm starting to worry that he's going to tell us that we have to wait twenty-four hours to report that Trish is missing."

"You're not filing anything, so that's not going to be an issue. Go see him and tell him what you just told me. He might know what's going on, and there's even a chance he knows why the Boxcar is closed."

"I'll try. What do you think about Rebecca? Could Grace and I have been so wrong about her?"

"It's not that hard to misread a clue," he said. "Don't beat yourself up about it. Gut reactions can be wrong sometimes. I'm speaking from experience here, because it's happened to me a time or two. Try not to let it get you down. As soon as I get back, I'll help you both look for Trish."

"Thanks for the offer, but who knows how long that will be? You've got problems of your own."

"That's why I'm calling. I just closed the case, and I'm on my way back to April Springs. I should be there in an hour."

"That's the best news I've had in a while," I said.

"Because you need my help?" he asked, fishing for a compliment.

"You can shorten that statement, if you'd like to. I need you. That's all there is to it, plain and simple."

"There's nothing plain or simple about it. I need you, too. Don't worry, between the three of us, we'll figure out what's going on."

My phone beeped, and I said, "Hang on a second, Jake. I've got another call."

I hit the button to put him on hold and said, "Hello?"

"Suzanne, this is Harry at the Pinerush Manor. You need to get over here as soon as you can."

"What's going on?"

"I just overheard Forrest on the telephone. He was in the garden, and it was pretty clear that he was under the impression that no one could overhear him, but I was just on the other side of the bushes. Someone's coming out here today, and I think it's going to be important."

"Why makes you think that?" I asked.

"I didn't hear much of the conversation, but I did hear him say, 'One way or the other, this is going to end today. Get out here as fast as you can, and we'll settle it once and for all.' Doesn't that sound significant to you?"

"We're on our way," I said.

I hit the button and brought Jake back up. "Sorry about that."

"I was beginning to think that you forgot about me."

"That's not going to happen," I said, and then I covered the mouthpiece and told Grace to drive to Pinerush.

"What was that?" Jake asked.

"We're headed to Pinerush," I explained. "Harry, the gardener, said that Forrest is up to something, and we want to find out what's going on over there."

"Is there any chance that you'll wait for me?" Jake asked.

"We would, but then we might miss whatever's going to happen."

There was a long pause, and then Jake asked, "Should I call in for some backup for you? I have a couple of friends in that area, and they both owe me a favor."

"No, we'll be fine. If we get in trouble, we'll call you."

"When do you think you'll get there?" he asked.

I glanced at the speedometer. "At the rate Grace is driving, it won't take that long."

"I'll be there as soon as I can. Don't take any chances until I get there, okay?"

"I'm not making any promises. Do me a favor, would you?"

"Anything," he said.

"Call Chief Martin and ask him about Trish. It might mean a little more if the question comes straight from you instead of from me."

"I'll do it right now. If I find out anything, I'll call you right back."

After I hung up, Grace asked me, "Do you really think it's all coming to a head right now?"

"It sounds as though Forrest is tired of playing around. I'm betting that he's going to make his move, but whether it's against Rebecca or Trish I can't say."

After a few moments of silence, she asked, "Is there any chance we should do what Jake asked and wait for him?"

"You heard that?" I asked.

"He doesn't exactly have a soft voice, does he? I heard everything he said to you. What do you think?"

"That maybe I should tell Jake to lower his voice whenever you're around."

"I mean about going to the manor without him," Grace explained.

"I knew what you meant. As much as I'd love to wait for an armed state trooper to show up to the rescue, we need to move fast. If we don't, we might lose our chance to save Rebecca. If we've already blown this and something has happened to Trish, I'm never going to be able to forgive myself, and I won't get involved in another murder investigation for as long as I live."

"You mean that, don't you?"

"I've never been more serious about anything in my life."

"Suzanne, if something did happen to Trish, and I don't think for one second that it did, there's no way you can blame yourself for it. We're doing the best we can."

"But what if it's not good enough?"

Grace let out a sigh, and then said, "Then we try harder the next time, but we don't give up. We never give up."

"Maybe," I said. I kept waiting for Jake to call back, but I'd just about given up hope when we finally pulled into the manor's long driveway.

"Should I call Jake and ask him if he was able to come up with anything?" I asked as we turned the corner.

"From the look of things, there's no time for that. What's going on over there, anyway?" Grace asked.

That's when I saw that an ambulance had pulled up in front of the main house, its lights flashing.

Something bad had clearly just happened at Pinerush Manor.

My Donuts as Easy as Pie Recipe

Again, I came up with this one while digging through my pantry. It's as easy as can be, and the donut holes are wonderful!

Ingredients
- 1 pouch muffin mix (we like Apple Cinnamon Martha White 7 oz. size)
- 1/2 cup whole milk
- Canola oil for frying (the amount depends on your pot or fryer)

Instructions
Stir the milk into the mix until moistened.

Drop bits of dough using a small-sized cookie scoop (the size of your thumb, approximately). Fry in hot canola oil (360 to 370 degrees F) 1 1/2 to 2 minutes, turning halfway through.

Yield: 10–12 donut holes

CHAPTER 17

"Are we too late?" I asked Grace as we rushed up the drive.

"I don't know," she said. She parked her car away from the ambulance, and we got out and raced toward it. Had Forrest already acted and beaten us to the punch? I couldn't take it if we were a little too late to help save another innocent victim.

Harry was out front watching the main door, and I doubted that he even realized we were there until I spoke to him.

"What's going on?" I asked, and he nearly jumped out of his skin.

"It's Mrs. Pinerush," he said.

"Was there an accident?" Grace asked. Could that have been who Forrest was going to settle up with when Harry overheard him? We might have missed identifying his next victim completely.

"What? No. She had trouble breathing, and Stephen called the paramedics."

"Do they know yet if she'll be all right?" I asked. I couldn't bear the thought of something happening to the older lady. Though Thomas Oak had told me that she was sick, it was still hard to reconcile that image with the strong woman I'd seen so recently.

"I overheard one of the EMTs say that she's on oxygen right now. They're taking her to the hospital to be sure she's okay, but this guy seemed hopeful."

They brought her out then. She was strapped to the gurney, and there was an oxygen tank at her side. I saw a thin tube running up to her face, and she looked really frail just lying there.

No one but Stephen and the EMTs were with her.

"Where's Forrest?" I asked as I looked wildly around. "Why isn't he here?"

"To be honest with you, in all of the commotion, I sort of lost track of him."

This was bad, very bad.

Where had he gone?

"I'm going to follow the ambulance to the hospital," Harry said, as Stephen approached us and said, "I'm going with you, Harry."

"That's fine by me," Harry answered, and then he turned to us. "Are you two coming?"

"We'll be right behind you," I said. Grace was a little surprised by my response, but she didn't say anything.

After they all pulled out, it left us at the manor alone. Grace asked me, "If we're following them, then why are we still here?"

"I want to see if Forrest is on the grounds before we go anywhere," I said. "There's nothing we can do to help Anne right now, and somebody else might be in trouble here."

"If he were anywhere around, wouldn't he be with his mother? I know full well that he might be a cold-blooded killer, but he wouldn't turn his back on her now, would he?"

"I don't know what he'd do, but I've got an idea that he's nearby. Did you see if Stephen locked the front door behind the EMTs?"

"There's only one way to find out," Grace said as we approached the front door.

It was open.

"What do you say? Are you ready to do a little trespassing?" I asked her.

"Funny, I seem to remember being invited in, don't you?"

I nodded. "Let's go see if we can track Forrest down and find out what's really going on."

Grace and I walked inside, and as we began searching through the rooms on the first floor for some sign of Forrest, I was more and more in awe of the great wealth the Pinerush family had accumulated over the generations. Elegant art hung from many of the walls in the rooms we entered, and priceless antiques were around every corner. In the study, I came across a display of antique pistols mounted over the fireplace that had to be worth more than everything I owned. The place looked more like a museum than a private residence, and I had to wonder if it might not have been kind of creepy growing up there as a kid. It was hard to believe that my friend the blacksmith had been raised in such posh surroundings.

"Suzanne, we could search all day and not find him. This place is huge."

"We have to at least try," I said. "Why don't you finish up here and I'll go start on the next floor?"

"No way. We're sticking together this time," she answered. In the past we'd both been caught alone at the worst possible times, and I had to admit that I was reassured by her presence beside me.

"Why don't we save the rest of this floor for later? I want to climb up and look out a few of the windows. Maybe we'll spot him somewhere out on the grounds."

We climbed the marble staircase and headed for the first window we saw. As Grace and I looked out onto the landscape, I spotted something out of place. "Grace, is that Rebecca Link's car over there?"

"Where?"

"Behind those bushes," I said as I pointed.

"It could be. Do you think that Forrest is settling the score with her right now?"

I kept scanning the land below us, and I finally caught a glimpse of something nearly out of sight on the edge of a nearby wooded area. It was a single flash of something red, and it was nearly gone as soon as I saw it, but then I got a better glimpse of it. As I watched, I saw that it was Rebecca's scarf. Even as I was about to tell Grace, I caught sight of Forrest as well.

The two of them were arguing, and it appeared that it was escalating by the second. What made things infinitely worse was that I spotted a handgun in Forrest's hand as it came into view.

"We need to stop him!" I shouted as I headed for the stairs, all the while pulling my cell phone out of my pocket.

"Who are you calling?" Grace asked as she followed me.

"Jake," I said, both in explanation to her and in response to my boyfriend answering his phone. "We're at the manor. Forrest and Rebecca are having some kind of confrontation out on the grounds in back."

"Don't do anything," he said. "I'll be there in ten minutes."

"We can't just hide so that we're safe inside," I shouted. "We have to stop him."

"Don't —" he said just as I hung up.

"We can't wait," I told Grace. "You know that, don't you? We have to stop him before he kills her, too."

"How are we going to do that?" Grace asked in desperation. "We're unarmed."

"We might be right now, but we can always bluff," I said as I dodged back into the study where I'd seen the old-fashioned revolvers over the fireplace.

I grabbed a gun for me and handed one to Grace as well.

"Where are the bullets?" she asked.

"I have no idea if these things even use shells," I said.

"What good are they, then?"

"I'm just hoping they buy us some time until Jake shows up," I confessed.

"But we know that Forrest is armed with a gun that actually has bullets in it."

"What can we do? We'll just have to sneak

up behind him and disarm him. I know it's not a perfect plan, but we can't just stand by and watch someone murdered while we're waiting for the infantry to show up. Grace, you don't have to do this if you don't want to."

"I'm going wherever you go," she said.

"Then let's do this before we lose our nerve, or something else bad happens out there."

We raced outside and did our best to hug the tree line so that Forrest wouldn't spot us coming. As we got within range, Rebecca saw us. Her eyes widened for just a moment, but she managed to kill her expression before Forrest caught on.

I was within three feet of him when my foot hit a fallen branch on the ground. As he started to turn at the sound of the snap, I rushed toward him and shoved the antique gun into his back so that he couldn't see my weapon. "Drop it, Forrest."

"You don't understand," he said.

"Shoot him! He wants to kill me!" Rebecca shouted.

"You're the murderer!" Forrest protested.

"If that's the truth, then who has the gun?" she yelled back.

At that moment, I wasn't entirely certain who to believe, but Rebecca's argument was a powerful one.

"This is the last time I'm going to tell you, Forrest. Throw your weapon over there, or I'm going to shoot."

Was he going to call my bluff, or do as I'd asked? I waited three heartbeats before I saw him start to lift the weapon. If he spun and fired at me now, I was dead, and I knew it.

After another moment of hesitation, he chucked the gun over into the woods.

At least now we were all unarmed.

"What happens now?" Forrest asked in a voice filled with resignation. "You've made a huge mistake, you know."

"My boyfriend will be here anytime," I said. "He can sort things out when he gets here."

"Jake's coming?" Rebecca asked.

"Even as we speak," I said.

That's when she dove for the gun.

Forrest had the same idea, but he was just a shade too late.

When Rebecca came up with it, I found that we were both staring down each other's barrels. "There's nothing you can do now. It's still a stalemate," I said.

Rebecca just laughed. "It might be if you knew how to load one of those pistols, let alone fire it. Those particular weapons haven't been fired in seventy-five years, I'm willing to wager."

"How can you be so sure?"

"I'm a bit of a gun nut. I thought for sure your friends from Napoli's must have told you. I saw them at the firing range just the other night."

That's when I remembered that Angelica had told me that a woman from April Springs had been at the shooting range in Union Square when we'd seen her there.

It was clear that Rebecca knew what she was talking about. Then again, if she *was* bluffing, I wasn't willing to call her on it.

I lowered my weapon and dropped it just as I heard Grace's fall near mine.

"There, now isn't that better?" she asked.

"Jake is still coming," I said.

"I doubt it. I think you're trying to bluff me again. What are you going to do, try to drag this out until someone notices that you're both gone and comes looking for you two?"

It would be in my favor for Rebecca to believe just that, so I dropped my head in defeat as I said, "You're right. He's not coming."

My captor smiled broadly at me. "I didn't think so. Now, who wants to go first? I believe we're going to have a little murder-suicide scenario here. Forrest, you're the murderer, so you go last. Suzanne, would you like to be his first victim, or should I shoot your best friend, Grace, first?"

"Shoot me," I said, nearly at the same time that Grace echoed the exact same words.

Rebecca found that amusing for some reason. "I get it. Friends to the end. You two really are BFFs, aren't you? It's just a shame that forever didn't last nearly as long as you must have hoped."

I took a step toward her, hoping to rush her before she could get more than one shot off. If I took the first bullet, it might allow Grace and Forrest a chance to escape into the nearby woods. The plan had the added bonus that if Rebecca didn't kill me outright, I might be able to wrestle the gun away from her. It wasn't much of a strategy, but it was all that I had.

The only problem was that I wasn't close enough yet.

I had to stall her until I could get close enough to limit the damage she could do.

"Why did you kill James, Rebecca? You're a pretty woman, and there are lots of other men in the world. Surely you could have found a replacement easily enough."

"Not like him," she said. "I begged him to

355

take me back, but he kept insisting that all he wanted was your friend Trish. I couldn't believe that I cried all of those tears for nothing."

"Did you already do something to Trish?" I asked. No matter what her answer was, I just had to know the truth before I died.

Rebecca scowled when she heard my question. "I tried to, but when I went by her diner today, I found out that she was closed for the day. She wasn't at home by the lake, either. Don't worry. I'll find her right after I finish with the two of you. She won't know what hit her."

"If you and James were fighting," I heard Grace ask, "how did you manage to get so close to him in the park? He had to be suspicious."

"That man was so naïve. I told him that I was sorry, and then I said that I wanted one last hug for old time's sake. As I moved close to him, I wrapped one arm around him as I drove the skewer into his chest with the other."

"What I can't figure out is how no one saw you do it," Grace said, her voice moving away from me. Was she planning to do something on her own? I had to move quickly now before she had a chance to act.

I wasn't about to let her save me if I could help it.

"I was as shocked as you were. After I stabbed him, he just stood there silently clutching his chest. I turned and started to walk away, and I was nearly back to my car when I heard the first scream. I saw you as you looked up from the donut shop, but you must not have seen me. I almost killed you that night, Suzanne, but I wasn't going to do anything until I could wrap up the rest of my loose ends."

"Why do you want to kill Forrest, though?" I asked.

"Go on. You can answer that better than I can," she said to her third captive.

"She was blackmailing me," he said simply. "James told her about something that I'd done in confidence, and the moment he was dead, she decided that it was time to collect."

"And you refused to pay her off?" Grace asked as I took another single step forward. I was almost there now.

"I forked over the money the first time," Forrest said. "But then she got greedy. I told her I wasn't going to pay her another dime, and she wouldn't allow it."

"Did your mother see what happened? Is

that why she left here in an ambulance?" I asked.

"What? What are you talking about?" he asked me.

"Your mother had some kind of attack. An ambulance came and got her, and she's in the hospital right now."

"Mother! What did you do to her?" Forrest yelled at Rebecca as he threw himself at her. She was as shocked as Grace and I were, and she took a step back as he dove toward her.

Just as the shot rang out, Grace and I tackled Rebecca from either side, and the gun went flying through the air. There had been no thoughts of escape from either one of us. Once again, I was proud to call Grace my friend, and I was even more thrilled that our relationship would live on past today.

Jake got there two minutes after Rebecca shot Forrest. He had his gun drawn when he came around the corner, and the moment he saw us, I yelled, "Jake, it's okay. I have her covered. She just shot Forrest, and she's the one who killed James."

"I'll call for an ambulance," he said, and did so as he continued to point his gun at Rebecca's heart. After he hung up, he barked at me, "Keep that pointed at her, too. If she so much as blinks, shoot her. Can you do that?"

"I'm ready and willing," I said, though in truth I wasn't sure that I'd be able to. Then again, if she threatened Jake or Grace, I had to believe that I could overcome my reluctance and do exactly as I'd been told.

Jake knelt down and applied a compress made out of his jacket to Forrest's chest.

"Is it bad?" Forrest asked as he lay there. "I can barely feel my chest."

"Give it a second," Jake said as he continued to apply pressure. "When it hits, it's going to feel like you've been kicked by a mule."

"Am I dying?"

"I don't think so," Jake said, "but then again, I'm not a doctor."

He started to try to get up, but Jake easily held him down with one hand. "Stay right where you are."

"But Mother is in trouble," he said. "I have to be with her."

In the distance we heard the ambulance sirens, so I said, "I think that's exactly where they're going to take you."

After the EMTs arrived and started taking care of Forrest, Jake took my hand and lowered the gun I was still holding on Rebecca. She had been surprisingly silent the entire time, and I had to wonder if she was in a state of shock herself. It was most likely one thing shooting at targets and silhouettes, but something else entirely when it was a real live person.

Jake cuffed her, and then he said to me, "Why don't you follow me to the local police station? I need to deliver this package, and then the two of you can give your statements, too, while we're there. Are you both up to it, or should we have you checked out at the hospital as well?"

"We're fine," I said. "Right, Grace?"

"A little jumpy maybe, but overall, I'm just peachy keen."

"Good. I'm glad you're both okay."

"Not as much as we are," I said.

I looked at the antique pistols still lying there in the grass and thought about retrieving them, but ultimately I decided to let someone else do it. I'd had my fill of guns for the moment, and I wasn't in any hurry to pick one up again anytime soon.

After Grace and I were finished with our statements, Jake met us in the hallway. "Are you all through?"

"We are," I said. "Now we just want to go home."

"I have to stick around a while, but I'll be

there shortly."

"Come to the cottage when you get back to April Springs," I said.

"You can count on it."

As we started toward Grace's car, he called out, "Aren't you both curious about what happened to Trish?"

"Rebecca told us herself that she was okay, at least she would be until she could get around to killing her. Why? Nothing happened to her, did it?"

"Nothing bad," Jake said. "It turns out that James's cousin came by the Boxcar and told her who he really was."

"I'm glad Rome came clean with her," I said. "What happened?"

"He wanted to hear all about the cousin he never knew. It turns out that the feud was between the fathers, not the sons. When Rome discovered how much of a kindred spirit James was, he wanted to hear everything there was to know about him. Trish agreed, and on a whim she decided to shut the Boxcar down so they could have some time to celebrate James's life, and his ideals."

"Funny, but that's what ended up saving her life," I said.

"James was a good man to the very end," Jake said.

As Grace and I drove back to April Springs, I had some time to reflect on just how many lives my friend the blacksmith had touched in his short time among us.

He would be missed by those who loved him, and honestly, what better legacy was there to leave behind? All of the wealth he'd inherited had done him no good in the end, but at least he'd had the satisfaction of knowing that his riches reached well beyond any bank balance or stock portfolio.

When it was my time to go, I only hoped that the same could be said about me.

The employees of Thorndike Press hope you have enjoyed this Large Print book. All our Thorndike, Wheeler, and Kennebec Large Print titles are designed for easy reading, and all our books are made to last. Other Thorndike Press Large Print books are available at your library, through selected bookstores, or directly from us.

For information about titles, please call:
   (800) 223-1244

or visit our Web site at:
   http://gale.cengage.com/thorndike

To share your comments, please write:
   Publisher
   Thorndike Press
   10 Water St., Suite 310
   Waterville, ME 04901